# ANNE CASSIDY

# MISSING JUDY

ing her,
ng walked off
out- gument. Her
ng to sister searched
ysit- her but could n
her anywhere.

local gir

GG

in-

SCHOLASTIC

Scholastic Children's Books,
Euston House, 24 Eversholt Street
London NW1 1DB, UK
a division of Scholastic Ltd
London ~ New York ~ Toronto ~ Sydney ~ Auckland
Mexico City ~ New Delhi ~ Hong Kong

First published in the UK by Scholastic Ltd, 2002
This edition published by Scholastic Ltd, 2006

10 digit ISBN 0 439 94998 X
13 digit ISBN 978 0 439 94998 9

Printed and bound by CPI Group (UK) Ltd, Croydon, CR0 4YY

10 9 8 7

# MISSING JUDY

# ONE

That day, when I saw my sister Judy again, was the day of the television programme. It was the first time in many months that her pale face and corkscrew curls had appeared in front of me. She was wearing her flowery skirt and the shocking-pink top that she'd begged Mum to buy for her. It was a colour that stood out among the greys and browns of the street; it seemed as though you could see it for miles.

There was the balloon as well, don't forget that.

I remembered it from eight years before. It was heart-shaped, made out of shiny pink plastic. It was filled with helium and bounced along proudly in the air, its ribbon hanging like a rakish tail. Judy had insisted on holding it herself and had given me sideways looks of disdain. I had spent my money on other things; stuff that had been eaten or read or used. I had nothing and she had the heart-shaped balloon.

It was after I'd finished college, and I saw the little girl getting off a bus. I focused on her face for a moment and then she turned away, the light from the afternoon sun bouncing off her curls. It made me swallow quickly and reach out to hold on to a nearby garden wall. My eyes clung to the tiny figure as she hopped off the bus platform and walked away. I saw her skirt and white trainers and a flash of the pink top from underneath a zip-up jacket. I stopped what I was doing and followed. Who wouldn't?

She was walking along with a woman, trailing behind, one of her feet kicking down into the pavement. I said *huh* quietly under my breath. She'd ruin the front of her trainers doing that. Mum had told her often enough. Then she hurried her steps and put her arm up to link with the woman. The balloon, not quite heart-shaped, was floating at half mast, tell-tale dimples in it where the gas had escaped. I quickened my pace, watching all the time for another glimpse of her face. I wanted to call out her name. *Judy*, I wanted to say, *Judy, come home with me.*

She went into a house with the woman and the front door shut sharply. I waited – what else could I do?

And then I remembered Pam, my counsellor. She'd be disappointed in me, I knew. She'd cut our sessions down and I was only seeing her once every month. She'd even talked about having a complete break to see how things went. I was busy, after all. I'd been at college for almost three months and was studying for A Levels. I even had friends and places to go in the evenings.

But my sister came first. Why was it that no one really understood that?

I looked keenly at cars driving by, hoping that Pam wasn't in one of them. I didn't want to be seen by her, or anyone for that matter, Mum or Dad even. And then it dawned on me. How could that girl be Judy? Even if she had a halo of brown curls and skin that was like double cream. Even if, hiding under that jacket, she was wearing a shocking-pink top. Even, I thought deflatedly, with the almost heart-shaped balloon trailing along behind her. She could not be my sister Judy.

My sister would be thirteen years old. Not a tiny girl of five.

She'd be big, maybe as tall as me. Her hair would probably be longer, possibly with some colour in it, blonde or red highlights. She'd be wearing make-up, I was sure, probably too much of it. Her clothes would be the latest designer labels or whatever she could persuade Mum and Dad to buy her.

Judy was good at that. Getting her own way with Mum and Dad. It helped being so pretty: all those curls bubbling around her face and that pale, pale skin, the colour of alabaster.

I wasn't jealous of her, no matter what Pam said.

That's why I waited outside that house. I stayed, standing in front of a garden wall on the opposite side of the road until long past dark. I was cold, I have to admit. My feet began to tingle and my fingers felt heavy inside my gloves. The lights went on in the houses around me and I saw a couple of curtains twitch.

It was on a road just like this that Judy had disappeared. Willow Drive. A street with houses along each side and trees dotted along the pavement. It was that time of day, too. Early evening, when everyone was having their tea. We should have been having ours. We shouldn't have been out at all.

But Judy had her own ideas. She'd walked off, her shoulders squared and her head high. She wouldn't wear a coat and the colourful top stood out. I saw a couple of heads turn at the little girl who was carrying the shiny balloon; no proper coat on such a cold night, it must have looked funny. *I'm going*, she said, *you can't tell me what to do.*

And I stood watching her walk away, her pink top making her stand out against the night, further and further up the street until she was swallowed up by the darkness. I never saw her again.

I've seen girls like her, girls that could be her twin; kicking their legs up on a swing in the park, queuing up at McDonald's, looking at the magazines in WHSmiths, buying an ice cream from a van parked by the side of the street.

That day, the day of the programme, I really thought it was her. It was the balloon that did it. Even though it wasn't pink, or heart-shaped, there was something about the sight of the girl's back moving ahead of me, her hand holding the balloon, that convinced me that this time I was right. That's why I ignored Pam's advice. I didn't pick my mobile phone from my pocket and press her number. I stood and waited, across the road, in case it was Judy, even though, in my head, I knew it wasn't.

Shining pink, puffed up with helium, she'd held it like a torch against the black night. When she vanished the balloon was found stuck in a tree. It had floated out

4

of her hand and the ribbon had become entangled in the branches. Something must have punctured it because it was flat, flapping in the wind. It must have looked like a broken heart.

That was all that was left of her.

A police car pulled up in front of me. There was no siren but the lights on the top were on and a WPC got out. She was stern at first and demanded to know what I was doing hanging around outside people's houses. When I explained who I was and why I was there her expression became cagey, as though she thought I might be taking the mickey out of her. She walked back over to the car and spoke to the other officer. There were some crackling sounds as they spoke on the radio. I looked away for a moment to see a couple of front doors open and people standing curious to find out who was being arrested. The door opposite, where the girl and her mother had gone in, was hanging open, the orange light from the hallway spilling into the front garden. The small girl was there, the one I had followed. I felt a jolt of disappointment when I realized that she was not my sister. She didn't look anything like her. I lowered my head and closed my eyes tightly.

The police took me home. The WPC recognized my mum straight away. She chatted with her while my dad put his arms around me and led me to the big armchair next to the radiator.

"Mrs Hockney, I'm sorry. I didn't link your daughter with..."

"That's all right," my mum said, waving her hand graciously.

My mum was wearing smart trousers and a blouse. She'd had her hair done, I noticed, and looked pretty, almost beautiful, I thought. Then I remembered that there were people coming round that night to watch the programme. The other members of the support group.

"I think your work is so important," the WPC was saying and my mum was nodding in that businesslike way that she has.

My dad was still in his bedroom slippers and looking at me in a troubled way. I noticed then that I was trembling with the cold. He rushed off and came back a few minutes later with a cup of tea that smelled as though it had alcohol in it. Out in the hall I could hear my mum saying goodbye to the policewoman. Her voice was distant; it sounded like it was a long way away.

*Kim took it badly. She never really got over it. She has counselling and we support her as much as we can.*

"I know what's triggered this," my dad's voice broke my concentration. He took my hands into his and rubbed them, "It's the programme, tonight. That's what's upset you."

He meant the documentary, LOST CHILDREN. Judy's case was one of many that was going to be reopened.

"Maybe," I whispered.

I tucked my feet up under me and hugged the hot tea, cringing at the heavy smell of brandy. I took a couple of gulps and pushed back into the chair. Looking round the room I saw some flowers in vases, and on the coffee table there were bottles of fizzy water and a tray with glasses standing neatly in a circle. In a while the members of the support group would arrive. Round-shouldered people who would creep into the living room and look apologetically about as though they really shouldn't be there.

My mum would float around taking coats, making coffee, pouring water, offering biscuits or sandwiches which no one would eat. There'd be a kind of smile on her face, the corners of her mouth turned up. My dad wouldn't do much at all. He'd sit in his chair, his bedroom slippers making his feet look sloppy and untidy. He'd wring his hands together and rub his neck nervously.

Someone, one of the parents of some other missing child, might say: *Kim's looking well! My, she's grown up! Isn't she growing into a pretty young lady!* And they'd all look at me and I'd feel myself blush at the intensity of their stares.

But it wasn't really me they were looking at. In my place was the ghost of my sister, Judy. Thirteen years old. Pretty, full of life, her curls vibrant, her skin like porcelain, all her life ahead of her. They'd all be thinking the same thing.

*If only Kim had looked after her that day eight years ago, she would still be alive.*

It was a cruel thing for anyone to think or say. But I couldn't argue with it, because it was true.

# TWO

Pam says I should always start at the beginning. The day when my sister went missing. Eight years ago, just after the half-term holidays when the clocks had moved back and the nights became suddenly darker. I was nine years old, and looking after Judy. Not that Mum had left me in sole charge. There were others around. It was just that I had the important task of amusing my sister for the whole afternoon.

Mum was busy helping Dad out. She was always busy in those days, working or at some meeting or shopping. She was often in a rush, searching for her files to pack into a bulky leather briefcase, always staring at her watch and dramatically saying *Is it that late?* as though there was a time bomb ticking quietly away in the corner.

She was big in those days. Overweight, some people called it, but she wasn't worried. She was fit and played badminton and when she wasn't supposed to be somewhere or meeting someone she often took Toby, our old dog, out for a walk. Judy nearly always went with her. I'd look out the window and see the two of them bobbing down the road, the dog slouching between them, Judy's face upturned to my mum, in the middle of some conversation or other.

I was happy to have some time to myself. I was one of those kids who liked my own company. I liked to read and write stories. I spent quite a few hours in my bedroom, tidying it up, sorting out my shelves and cupboards. I had my best friend, Teresa Russell, who lived a few streets away. She was an only child whose mum didn't work, and her house was always tidy and quiet. Her clothes were always ironed and hung up, her things put away into cupboards that had labels made out of bubble writing. I wanted to be like her.

Looking after my sister was not my favourite activity. For a start she talked non-stop. She would tell you everything that had happened to her that day; who did what to whom, how she felt about it, what they should have done, what she would have done in their place. I usually nodded and ummed and let her rattle on.

She also worried a lot about pointless things.

"Kim, what happens when all the land, across all the world, is full up with houses? Where will people live then?"

"What would happen if it rained and rained and never stopped?"

"Where do all the pigeons live, Kim?"

I used to give her any old answers just to shut her up. You had to do that with Judy. If you gave her any encouragement she'd be talking to you for hours. My dad said she could talk for England. Whenever he took her to his shop she'd sit on the counter and interrogate the customers. *Judy Chatterbox*, that's what her teacher called her. She was sweet and friendly and she'd talk to anyone. That's what my mum and dad said at the first press conference. *Talk to her*, they said. *You'll see. She loves a conversation.*

On the Saturday afternoon, when it happened, my mum wanted to go to Lakeside Shopping Centre. She needed a new coat, she said. Judy was going to go with her. She was delighted and had dressed up in her newest clothes: her skirt, white trainers and a shocking-pink fleece top that had cost far too much money the previous week. She was parading around the house looking at herself in all the mirrors.

I didn't want to go to Lakeside. My mum was going to drop me off at Teresa's house and we were going to play with a jewellery kit that she had. We were going to make matching necklaces and bracelets. After that her mum was going to let us cook jam tarts. I'd been looking forward to it since school on Friday afternoon when the arrangements had been made.

My dad was in the shop, as usual, and Toby was lying in the corner of the hall, his ear flicked inside out, his legs taking up all the space at the bottom of the stairs.

Just after lunch, as we were getting ready to go, my mum got a phone call from my dad. Grace Peters, the woman who worked on the till in his shop, had stumbled down the stairs and broken her ankle. He wanted my mum to get in the car and take Grace to Casualty so that he could keep the shop open. It was Saturday afternoon, a busy time for a baker's.

My mum was angry. I heard her sounding off on the telephone.

"I work all week. I need one day to myself. Is that too much to ask? What about an ambulance? Hasn't Grace got anyone who can take her?"

As I came out of my bedroom I heard the receiver being dropped noisily into place and several mumbling, grumbling sounds. Moments later my mum's voice marched ahead of her up the stairs.

"Kim, you'll have to take Judy with you to Teresa's. I'm sure her mum won't mind."

The plans had to be changed. There were to be no arguments. It was nobody's fault. Poor Grace Peters was in a terrible state, she said. They would go to Lakeside the next day and Teresa's mum wouldn't mind a bit. She liked Judy.

Judy gave me a little smile. She had put on her chain with the letter "J" on it that she was allowed to wear at weekends. She was holding it out from her neck and then sliding the "J" into her mouth. It was something that Mum was always telling her off about but she looked cocky and full of herself. Spending the afternoon with me and Teresa, *the big girls*, was a real treat. For me it promised a few hours of deep irritation.

Afterwards, I remembered vividly that time after Dad's phone call, when everything was still normal. It took us about ten minutes to get ready. We put our coats on and Mum turned the lights off in the kitchen and locked the back door. These were routine, everyday things. Getting into the car Judy piped up with her usual request, *Can I sit in the front?* even though it wasn't her turn. None of us knew that we were doing these things for the last time ever. My mum was in a flap and I was fed up about the fact that Judy was going to be with me and Teresa all afternoon. Only Judy was cheerful, singing along with a song on the radio. We got out of the car at Teresa's and waved as Mum drove off. In my hand was a five-pound note. I was to spend it on treats for the three of us. It was a sort of apology for the broken arrangements. It sat in my back pocket and lifted my spirits a bit, I have to admit.

About six the three of us went out to spend it. Me and Teresa bought a magazine and some sweets. Judy wanted the heart-shaped balloon. It cost more than her fair share so we hummed and hawed. She made such a fuss that in the end I let her have it. Teresa got into a strop and went ahead, in the direction of her own house.

Then Judy walked off in a huff. I stood awkwardly, holding the coat that she had refused to wear. I didn't know what to do. A couple of people across the street were getting out of their car and they watched her walking away. She was only five and she shouldn't have been on her own, I knew that, but she was so headstrong. *You can't tell me what to do*, she said. To tell the truth I was angry with her. I waited for ages; I counted at least ten cars go by. I looked round from time to time to see if Teresa was coming back, but she didn't. I kept walking a few steps this way and that, peering into the darkness to see if I could pinpoint my sister.

I could see my breath in the air and I began to feel terribly cold. I was standing underneath a streetlamp. I didn't have a watch on so I had no idea of the time. I decided to walk in the direction that she had gone. I thought she might be playing a game or hiding and I was half expecting her to jump out and try and frighten me. I braced myself for the surprise as I strode along the dark street looking around me all the time for any sign of her.

At the end of Willow Drive I looked up and down the next road. There was just a yawning blackness. No Judy, no flash of pink, no balloon. An awful feeling settled in my stomach and my head was low as I walked back up the street and in the direction of Teresa's house. All the time I was thinking, *She'll be there at Teresa's when I get back. My mum'll be there as well. It'll be me they're worried about, not Judy, because she'll be standing holding that stupid balloon, shivering a bit, waiting for me to give her back her coat.*

I could see my mum's car parked outside Teresa's and a shape at the living-room window looking out. As I got there my mum flew out of the front door and looked happily at me and then behind me and around me, her eyes falling here and there on the empty street, her face puzzled.

"Where's Judy?" she said.

Behind her I could see Teresa and her mum. But no Judy.

"Where is she?" my mum said, her voice quite normal, as if she expected a normal kind of answer.

"I don't know," I said, the words stuck in my throat.

"It'll be all right." I could hear Teresa's mum's voice. "They've had a quarrel. She'll be along in a minute."

My mum pulled her car keys out of her pocket. She rattled them about a bit and looked as though she was thinking hard. Then she took my shoulder and gently guided me towards Teresa and her mum.

"I'll drive round. I'll pick her up. I won't be long."

I watched the car drive off, its headlights lighting up the gardens opposite for a few moments. Then it was gone. I heard Teresa's mum whisper something to Teresa and then she was at my shoulder, her hand resting on my neck.

"She'll find her. That little Miss Chatterbox will be back any minute."

How I longed for that. To hear my sister talking again – but instead of chatter there was only silence.

# THREE

There wasn't a single empty seat in the living room when the programme started. I was still sitting in the armchair near the radiator and my dad was on the floor in front of me. My mum and a couple of her friends from the support group were on the settee. The others were on the wooden dining-room chairs that were dotted around. My Aunt Rosie was there as well, her knitting needles clicking rhythmically, my Uncle Jeff beside her.

Up to that point the room had been full of talk: people saying hellos to each other, chatting about what they'd done since their last meeting. Even though I wasn't especially looking at any of them I could hear their words.

"You've put a bit of weight on, my dear. You look so much better for it."

"I saw that interview in the paper with your husband. Very good stuff. Not at all sentimental."

"We've spent the summer in Australia, with my brother and his wife. It did us good to get away..."

It was like the beginning of a party, a wedding or a christening. People catching up on each other's lives. No one mentioned the missing children, the main reason that they were there. They sat around my living room with their hands gripping the arms of chairs, thin smiles barely covering expressions of desolation, the buzz of cheerful conversation drowning out the terrible absence of children's voices.

In the middle of it all I heard my Aunt Rosie.

"The nursery is doing quite well. This summer we sold more than ever. Those big Grecian pots were really popular. And hanging baskets. We were so busy."

My Uncle Jeff nodded in agreement, picking up the tiny glass of whisky that was by his side. There was some umming and people joined in, talking about plants and flowers as though they were grateful for a new subject. I looked hard at my aunt and uncle. I wondered if they were feeling uncomfortable. Among the dozen or so people in the living room they were the only ones who hadn't had a child taken away from them.

When the programme started there was a sudden hush, like a heavy door closing. The silence was dense and I knew that all eyes were boring into the television screen. My dad's shoulder became hard against my leg and I could almost see his muscles tensing.

It opened with some heavy music and pictures of children playing. A park scene with boys and girls on swings and climbing frames; a street scene showing youngsters on bikes and skateboards; a school playground where a group of girls were playing a game of hopscotch. The children were young, all under ten, I'd say, and they were laughing and shouting and hugging each other; some were chewing gum or eating chocolate or taking swigs from bottles of drink. Then, one by one, the scenes froze and the word MISSING appeared across each of them as though it had been rubber-stamped. I felt a silent gasp among the people there in the room beside me. I looked around; all of them were taut, their faces frozen in concentration. My Aunt Rosie had stopped knitting, her needles resting in mid-air for a moment. Only my mum looked serene. Her back straight, she seemed to gain in height on the settee. Maybe it was because the others were sinking down into the cushions, their plates of biscuits perched dangerously on the arm of the chair.

Then the programme began. The commentator started talking about the statistics and then showed photos of each of the four missing children who were to be discussed on the programme that night. My sister Judy was the second to be shown. When her picture came on to the screen I stopped noticing what was going on in the room around me and found myself sucked into the television, unable to take my eyes off the screen.

*Judy Hockney was only five years old when she went missing on a cold November afternoon eight years ago. She was a bright, talkative child, not at all shy. She was with her sister, Kim, on the afternoon that it happened.*

I felt the familiar heaviness in my stomach. My dad looked up at me and smiled.

*After a quarrel with her sister she walked off and was*

*never seen again. Her mother, Maureen Hockney, searched the streets for her daughter for about fifteen minutes. Then she rang the police. Local officers and neighbours did house-to-house searches and at first light the following morning the nearby river was searched by police frogmen. There was no trace of Judy.*

They cut to a shot of the first press conference that my mum and dad had given. My mum was fatter then and she did most of the talking. My dad nodded a few times but he said nothing.

*"Our daughter Judy is a friendly girl. Talk to her and you'll see. She loves a conversation."*

My mum was looking straight at the screen, her eyes straining to focus on something, as though she could see through the camera and into the living rooms of all the people watching her instead of the other way around. She seemed to be *talking directly* to a particular person.

*"She's a sweet person and we're asking you to give her back to her family. You can do that. You can leave her outside a hospital or some shopping centre. No one ever needs to know."*

All the time there were flashes of light as the cameras took their front page photographs.

*"Please give her back,"* my mum ended by saying. Then she turned to my dad as if for some support. He just bowed his head though, and a policeman nearby put his hand up to call a halt to the press conference.

I knew nothing of this at the time. After my mum got into her car and drove off from Teresa's house I stayed and waited for news. Mrs Russell was very kind and kept saying positive things.

"She'll be at the sweetshop. She'll be at one of her friend's houses. She'll have gone home in a huff. She'll turn up at the bread shop."

We made the jam tarts, I remembered. Teresa's mum cleared the table and gave us half of the pastry each. We had to sprinkle the flour on the surface so that the pastry wouldn't stick to the rolling pin. We had to grease the trays and then spoon the jam into each tart.

The kitchen was bright and warm against the dark outside. There was a radio playing and Teresa's mum seemed to keep talking the whole time we were there. After a while the smell of the pastry cooking filled the room. We got some plates ready for the tarts. There was an air of normality, as though nothing terrible could happen. When the phone rang she raised her eyebrows at me as if to say, *Now we'll see where the little chatterbox got to.*

Me and Teresa stood by the banisters. Her mum's voice started off brightly and then got lower and lower, her words at a minimum, just *ums* at the end. When she replaced the receiver she stood for a moment in silence as though she didn't quite know what to say. Teresa was standing very close to her, as if to claim ownership. I stood looking at them, a terrible feeling snaking through my insides. In the air was the faint whiff of something burning.

"The tarts!" she said, running into the kitchen.

They were not burned, just crispy. Nobody wanted any. They sat on a plate, untouched.

"Poor Judy must have got lost," Teresa's mum said. "Your mum and dad have been down to the police station. The police are going to help look for her!"

She took my hand.

"Your mum wants you to stay over tonight. And in a little while a police lady will come and talk to you about Judy."

I must have stiffened because she crouched down by my chair and rubbed my arm.

"Everything will be fine. This police lady, she just wants to ask you what happened. She wants you to point out the place where you last saw little Judy."

I nodded. When the policewoman arrived my dad was with her. He hugged me and looked cheerful. He said everything would be all right. I took them to Willow Drive, to the very spot where Judy had walked off. I pointed out the direction that she'd gone. I showed them how I'd followed her to the corner and looked up and down. They both kept saying *Good, good, very good.* As though I was passing some kind of test. I kept asking them where Mum was and Dad said that she was having *a little lie-down*, which at the time I thought was strange.

Dad gave me a big hug and said I should be a good girl while they looked for Judy.

I did try to be a good girl. I sat beside Teresa and watched a video while her mum fluttered in and out of the room bringing drinks and sweets and asking us if we were warm enough. Later on I found out that her dad had gone out to help with the search. I never saw him come in, though, because Teresa's mum had us both tucked up in her double bed. She said we could keep the light on if we wanted. It was gone midnight but she even allowed us to listen to one of Teresa's taped books on a tiny cassette.

My best friend, Teresa, was quiet, her eyes darting this way and that. Her mum was making a real fuss of me and I noticed a couple of times how Teresa inserted her thumb between her lips and started to suck it. Neither of us mentioned Judy the whole evening. We both acted as though nothing had happened.

Then, when we were both lying back, surrendering to tiredness, our eyelids drooping, she shook my shoulder and spoke softly.

"Do you think Judy might be dead?"

I lay very still, hardly breathing. My eyes stared at her until they lost focus. I felt my face heating up and my throat contract with misery. I reached out to her but Teresa snapped the lamp off and I was left lying in the dark staring into a black hole.

My dad collected me the next morning and I didn't see Teresa Russell again for many months.

The programme was coming to an end. My dad had got

up and gone out to the kitchen to put the kettle on. There was some wriggling about and a few whispered comments.

"The important part is coming on now," my mum said.

I focused back on the screen. I wondered why the production team had chosen to include my sister's story. The case had been exhaustively pursued by the police. It had featured on *Crimewatch* and similar TV programmes. The local newspapers had reported on the case from time to time: MISSING JUDY – THE FIRST ANNIVERSARY. THREE YEARS ON. FIVE YEARS AND NO CLUE.

My mum was sitting bolt upright, one leg crossed over the other. My dad had come back into the room and was leaning against the door jamb. There was an air of tension in the room, my Aunt Rosie laying her needles down and grabbing my uncle's hand. On the screen I could hear some mumbling about computer technology aiding the search for missing people. I looked to see what was coming. The presenter was standing by a giant computer screen talking to a small man with frizzy hair. He was wearing rimless glasses and kept nervously adjusting them and frowning, not knowing whether to look at the camera or the presenter. In the end he turned to the computer monitor and pointed.

"Are you saying," the presenter said, "that we can actually see what these children might look like if they were alive today?"

"Hypothetically speaking," the man with glasses said. "We work on the last photographs taken of the missing child. We factor in the physical characteristics of the parents and the number of years that the child has been missing. The computer produces an image that could be that of the grown-up individual. Judy Hockney is a very good example of this. She was five when she disappeared. There is no evidence that she is dead. If she were alive today the computer has suggested that she might look like this."

Both men stood back from the screen as an image came up. The face of a teenage girl looked out. My mum let out a tiny sound

It was like looking at a photograph. It was Judy's eyes in a different face. A grown-up face. Her skin smooth, she was smiling, just as she had done in all the photographs that we had of her. She had more teeth, none of the gaps that she'd had as a tiny child. Her face was longer, most definitely; her hamster cheeks thinned out so that in adolescence she had cheekbones. Her hair hung around her face, wavy rather than curly. It was mid-brown, perhaps a little red.

It was my sister. For eight years I had not seen her, and here she was, in my living room, looking straight at me.

# FOUR

After everyone had gone, the three of us, my mum, my dad and me, sat down and watched the programme again on video. We fast-forwarded the sections on the other children and just concentrated on the bit about Judy. I was sitting on the settee beside my mum. She had a notepad in her hand and a pen. My dad was in the armchair over by the radiator. He had a tea towel in his hands from where he'd been drying up the dishes.

This time I took more notice of the presenter and the things he said. He talked about the main leads that the police had followed up.

"*The police did a thorough house-to-house on the streets where Judy went missing. They looked at CCTV footage on the main roads and the nearby roundabout. They put out descriptions of the girl and her clothes. A reconstruction of the girl's last movements was carried out.*"

The presenter was trying to make it sound dramatic. His words were loud and soft and he left gaps to allow tension to build up "... the girl's LAST movements ... was ... *carried out*". He was almost whispering by the time he got to the end of the sentence. The next things they showed were items of clothing identical to those worn by my sister. The flowery skirt, the trainers and the pink fleece top. My mum was taking notes, writing furiously as though she hadn't heard every detail of this a thousand times before. My dad had folded the tea towel up into a tiny square and he was pinching at its corners.

"The big break," the presenter said, in a punchy way, as if he meant business, "was the information about the red van..."

The red van. I had almost forgotten it. I held my breath and felt my ribs tightening around my chest. A photograph of a red van appeared on the screen. I looked at my mum. She had stopped writing. The presenter's voice sounded.

*"It wasn't until a week after Judy's disappearance that the report of a red van came to light. An eyewitness said that the van passed close by the scene at the time of Judy's disappearance. The witness remembered some letters from the registration number. An X and a P. A nationwide search followed, which used the latest technological developments in police computers."*

Some footage was shown of police staff sitting in front of computer monitors. All the while I watched I found myself scratching the inside of my arm. It was a nervous reaction to stress, I knew, Pam had explained it to me. *Take deep breaths*, she'd said. *Count backwards from twenty. Don't stop until you get to one.* I didn't have time, though, because we'd reached the bit of the programme where Judy's picture was shown. My mum put her pad and pen down and leaned forward on the seat.

The computer image of my sister looked out from the

television again. Her face was pretty, and pleasing to look at. She had a slight smile as though something mildly amusing had just occurred to her. Her hair flicked loosely around her face. The computer expert pointed to her hair and said that it could be shorter, longer or even a different colour.

He was talking about Judy as though she was still alive. It gave me this feeling in my chest like the fluttering of a bird's wings. This was something I'd thought and thought about. I knew, without asking, that my mum and dad thought it as well. It was never mentioned though, never spoken about. Because Judy's body had never been found we each held a tiny seed of hope that she was living somewhere else, alive and well. For eight years there had been no gruesome discoveries, no lifeless form fished out of a river, no shallow grave disturbed by a dog or wild animal. Judy had simply vanished into thin air. We didn't have her, it was true, but we couldn't be sure that she was dead either.

Mum spoke suddenly, her words loud and firm.

"She would have been tall, I'm sure. And athletic. I'll bet she would have liked sports."

My dad and me both looked at her with surprise. She coughed lightly and let her head drop. My mum rarely talked about Judy any more. Oh, she *discussed* her in her support group, as a case study or as an example to new members. She would give out statements to the press if they rang asking for a comment on some new law or development in police procedure. But she never mentioned her as a person any more.

How long had it been like that? Two years? Three? Nearer to five?

My dad stood up. He put the tea towel on the arm of the chair and came across to the settee. He knelt on the floor in front of my mum and took the notepad off her. He put one arm out to me and I grabbed his hand. Then he buried his head in my mum's chest. I closed my eyes for a few minutes. I felt like I was in a church in the middle of a prayer. Then, when I heard my mum's sobs, like tiny hiccups bursting out of her, I got up and walked out of the room leaving them alone together.

I went up to my room with heavy footsteps. I unpacked my college things, my files and books that I'd carried with me when I followed the young girl home from the bus stop. I saw then the absolute stupidity of it. Every ounce of common sense I had told me that that little girl wasn't Judy, and yet I'd let myself be drawn along, pulled as if by some invisible thread. I must have looked an idiot, maybe even some sort of nutter.

It wasn't as if it was the first time. Wasn't that why Pam had appeared? To help me come to terms with it? To stop me making a public nuisance of myself?

I picked up my mobile phone and saw, on the screen, a small envelope. I pressed the buttons to bring up the missed message and immediately wished that I hadn't bothered. It was from Teresa Russell. SAW THE PROG. POOR JUDY. I DO THINK ABOUT HER, LOVE TESSA.

I deleted the message and didn't reply.

Later, when I was getting ready for bed, memories of the past, things I hadn't thought about for a long time, came into my head. *Let the past trickle through. Don't fight it*, Pam had said to me. I knew that the programme was to blame. Like a stone splashing into water, it had stirred everything up. Pictures and feelings floated up to the surface of my mind and I sat back and let them swim before me.

The first few days after Judy disappeared, the three of us spent most of our time sitting in the living room being fed cups of tea and sandwiches by a couple of plain-clothes police officers, a man and a woman, Beth and Rob, both of whom who were *experienced* in situations such as ours. When they weren't trying to feed us they tidied up, took phone calls, answered the front door, walked the dog. At the first sign of upset they sat down and held our hands, hugged us, spoke soothingly; once or twice they cried themselves. All the time they talked softly; about the house, the street, my dad's shop, my mum's job, my school and – if we wanted – they talked about Judy.

Although my mum and dad attended a couple of press conferences, I never left the house. I spent a lot of my time sitting with Toby, grooming him, trying to get him to play. After I'd told the uniformed police officers everything I knew they left me alone for a couple of days. When Judy didn't turn up they came back. They talked quietly to Beth and Rob, their hands covering their mouths, their eyes sliding across the room to where I was sitting. Then they left, the front door closing softly behind them. That's when Beth would take me into the back room and chat quietly to me, going over everything that happened. Time and time again. *Are you sure you don't mind talking about it?* she'd say. Sometimes Rob was there. They had photographs of Willow Drive. Some in broad daylight and some at night. Beth would point to everything in the picture and we'd talk about it. *Just chatting*, she'd say. *You never know what might come out of your memory that way.* She pointed to each house. *Did I know who lived there? Did anyone come out or go in while I was standing watching Judy?* I couldn't tell them anything new. And they were so nice I felt bad about disappointing them.

On the third day, with my mum sitting next to me, they showed me a series of photographs of men's faces. These were men who had shown interest in children in the past. I wasn't sure exactly what that meant but I looked carefully anyway. They were older, greasy-looking faces, with dull eyes. Some were bald, some had grey hair, one or two had glasses. Had I seen any of these men hanging round? In the previous days? In the shop where we'd gone to spend our money?

My answer was always no. Beth and Rob gave me cheerful smiles. My mum gave me a hug and then sat looking through the photographs herself, studying each one voraciously.

Then we looked at pictures of different types of cars and lorries and vans. Did any of them look familiar?

Might one of them have driven past me at speed on the night that Judy disappeared? Maybe moments after? I shook my head and watched their faces drop.

I was letting them all down.

That's why I told them about the red van.

It was during the reconstruction, exactly one week after it happened. My mum and dad stayed at home, but Beth took me in a car to watch the proceedings. *In case it jogged my memory*, she said hopefully. The police had got two young girls to re-enact the disappearance, daughters of one of the officers. One was older, like me (even though she looked nothing like me); the other was five, wearing the same clothes that Judy had worn and clutching the heart-shaped balloon. They stood in the dark street at exactly the same time that Judy and I had been there. The street was full of photographers and some members of the public. The police seemed quite pleased by this. Beth explained it to me.

"We're hoping to reach people who might only walk down or drive around these streets once a week. They may have heard about Judy on the TV but they may not link the scene of the disappearance with somewhere they regularly go. The same with motor cars. We have officers stopping people as they drive by. They'll point the little girl out to them and ask them if they remember anything. You'd be surprised how much good, strong evidence we've come up with in similar cases."

"Could we walk along behind?" I said.

"No, I don't want the press taking pictures of you. We

could drive up to the next road, though."

We drove round in a loop and parked beyond Willow Drive. The small girl was walking towards us, followed by police and photographers. She had a smile on her face which chilled me. I looked up and down the street where we were parked. There were policemen and women stopping cars and passers-by. They were talking animatedly and taking names and addresses. I knew this because Beth had told me. There was an air of excitement, as though something was going to happen. Beth was tapping her fingers on the steering wheel, hardly breathing.

"Someone will remember something," she whispered, and put her hand over mine. "You watch, something will turn up."

She was so nice, so kind. She had worked so hard all week looking after us. Mum and Dad had moved between the settee and sleep while she and Rob had done absolutely everything. She had even bathed Toby's eyes and sat up with me in the middle of three or four nights when I couldn't sleep. She was desperate to help, to find a clue. And I wanted so much to please her. So I told her about the red van.

"I'm sure I saw it passing by," I explained, "when I followed Judy and looked round this corner."

I pointed to a place across the road, a few metres from where I had been standing, looking hopelessly up and down the road, searching for Judy. Beth looked at me with wonder.

"The reason I remember," I said, "is that it didn't slow down over the speed hump. It kind of jumped up in the air."

"Did it?" Beth said, reaching for her radio.

There were other police officers and more questions. This time I didn't feel so bad answering them. This time I had something to say. Was it an old van? A new van? Neither, I thought, closing my eyes to picture it. Dusty, I thought, as though it needed a good wash. Did I know the type? *No, of course not. How could a nine-year-old be expected to know the type of van?* I didn't know the type, I agreed, but I did remember some of the letters on the registration. X and P.

*That was it*, I said, *I couldn't remember any more.*

*Good girl! Excellent! Well done!* They were so pleased. There was a hum of activity in the street, the police talking in little huddles, the press taking notes down. When we got back to the house Beth announced it as though we'd just won the lottery. *Kim has remembered something very important*, she said. *It's a major clue and it could lead to something.*

After that the investigation was centred round the red van and the search for it. Using the two letters I had given them, they investigated thousands of vans and their owners.

They found nothing. No van and no Judy.

I heard a knock on my door which shook me out of my thoughts. Feeling dazed, I looked around the room and then at the clock. It was almost midnight. The door opened a few centimetres and my mum stood there.

"I just wanted to make sure you were all right," she said, walking across and sitting down beside me.

Her face was blotched and she looked tired. She took my hands in hers.

"This programme," she whispered, "might be just the thing to jog people's minds. If we could only find out what happened, then we could have closure."

*Closure*. It was a new word – American, I knew. It meant that we could close a door on the events of the past and get on with our lives. For that to happen we needed to know what had happened to Judy. Only then could we stop looking back over our shoulders.

"We'll see what happens. Maybe it will register with someone. Maybe there'll be new clues."

She gave me a kiss on the cheek and then left. The door closed snugly behind her. New clues. Like the red van. The most important clue of the whole investigation.

Except that it wasn't true. I had made it up to please a nice policewoman. When Judy disappeared the streets were empty and quiet. There never was a red van.

# FIVE

The following Monday my friend Clare gave me a lift to college. She was driving her mum's car and tooted her horn lightly when she pulled up outside my house. My dad was still in bed but my mum was up and dressed and working on the computer.

Clare had to move her portfolio from the passenger seat into the back so that I could sit down. On the floor was her rucksack full of art paraphernalia. I didn't bother to move it. I just slipped my feet in to the available space and rested my own bag on my knee.

"Saw the programme on Friday," she said, looking back over her shoulder and moving out from the pavement at a snail's pace.

I nodded tightly, not really wanting to talk about it. The car crept up the street, juddering a little as we went round the bend. With a bit of fiddling about Clare produced a tape and stabbed it into the player. The car was full of music and I sat back gratefully, glad to avoid any discussion about my family.

I had met Clare when I started college three months before. She was one of the students assigned to show the new first years around. She studied Art and was in her second year. Her hair was jet black and always had some coloured strands depending on the paints she was working with. She was fairly untidy-looking and didn't seem to care whether her clothes were ironed or her face was clean. She had an air of distraction about her, as if her mind was always somewhere else. To tell the absolute truth, this suited me. Close friendship was not something I felt comfortable with.

After Teresa Russell and I stopped spending time together I drifted a bit. I had friends, but never anyone who was what you might call a *best friend*. It took a long time for me to get back to school, and when I did I was a bit of a curiosity to everyone. Some kids were very friendly, oozing with unspoken sympathy. Others were downright nosey and wanted to know what it felt like to have quite literally lost a sister. I tended to steer clear of either sort. For this reason I usually ended up hanging round with lads. With them it was simple. You played a bit of football or swapped cards or talked about television. You didn't worry about people's feelings or their histories. There were other girls like this, as well, and when I was fed up with the boys I usually ended up palling around with them. I never got close to anyone again. It suited me.

Teresa Russell went to a different secondary school and I hardly ever saw her. Occasionally we would pass each other in the street or at the shopping centre. Both of us would manage a curt nod. I didn't like her any more, it was as simple as that. Pam had her theory, of course. Teresa was a reminder to me of that fateful afternoon. Every time I saw her I remembered losing Judy. It was laughable. It supposed that I wasn't remembering Judy all the time anyway. No, I just saw Teresa Russell for what she was – selfish and manipulative.

So, after five years of secondary school, I was dismayed to run into her at Sixth Form College. She was doing a Business Studies course and I was doing History, Media and English A levels so we didn't see much of each other. She had a boyfriend who was doing the same course and she always seemed to have her arm linked in his; either that or you stumbled over the two of them snogging in a corner of the canteen or some shadowy corridor. When she first saw me she acted like we were long-lost friends. She made a big fuss and introduced me to the boyfriend, Danny. When I turned to walk away I felt the hairs on the back of my neck standing up. I knew she was talking about me, telling him all the stuff about my sister. I had a sort of notoriety and she revelled in it.

Clare was the opposite. Clare knew who I was the minute we met.

"You're the kid who lost her sister?" she said, showing me the computer room and the library (latest technology, very convenient, masses of books).

I'd nodded, surprised by her forthright manner.

"That's awful," she said. "Was it a long time ago?"

We moved towards the college theatre (stepped seating, proscenium stage, state-of-the-art lighting).

"Almost eight years," I said, quietly, not wanting the other students to hear.

"I'll bet you think about her every day. I know I would."

I nodded gratefully as she pointed out the canteen (overcrowded, like a sauna, crap food, hardly any veggie choices).

Her honesty had shaken me. She wasn't embarrassed or impressed, just *interested*. After that I used to see her around and we'd have coffee or just sit and chat. She hardly mentioned it again. She told me that my surname was the same as one of our greatest painters, David Hockney. I hadn't known this, but it seemed to give us a strange link. She was always talking about her course, her pictures, collages, sculptures. As well as that she was interested in weird things: reincarnation, stone circles, pagan festivals, meditation. Through it all she was warm and friendly and didn't make me feel that she was spending time with me because I was from a famous family.

She had problems of her own. Her family was in upheaval. Her mum and dad were separated and her mum's new boyfriend, a computer programmer or analyst or something, had moved in a couple of months before. Clare quite liked him, but whenever her dad visited there were arguments between the two men and she found herself in the middle of them. She occasionally came into college with puffy eyes, looking more dishevelled than usual. The artwork she did was downright odd. Her paintings were dark and messy, the figures in them disproportionate, with big heads and tiny bodies. Her art teachers loved her work. Clare just got on with it.

She had no time to feel sorry for me.

When we got to college she rushed off to a lecture and I went to an English lesson.

In class we were looking at *the language of the leaflet*. The tables were covered in piles of colourful leaflets, all shapes and sizes. Our task was to put them into different categories. I was sitting with a lad who was flicking through a magazine and a couple of girls who had been in my secondary school. After some analysis we were going to prepare our own leaflets. We set about our task, a couple of the girls talking about the TV soaps while we were doing it. I was only half listening.

Writing a leaflet was nothing new to me. My mum and dad produced masses when they set up the support group, CHILDLOSS. I'd helped to devise and set out leaflets, as well as newspaper advertisements and press statements. By the age of twelve I could have worked in PR.

On the first anniversary of Judy's disappearance my mum and dad and me walked along Willow Drive and placed flowers against a tree. We did it early in the morning; about seven o'clock when there was no one around. My mum spent some minutes tying the bouquet to the trunk of the tree. In amongst the flowers, covered in plastic, was a small photo of Judy. It was the head-and-shoulders shot that the police had used for their publicity. We all stood quietly for a few minutes, then we turned and walked back.

"We should get in touch with other parents," my dad said when we had almost reached home.

My mum automatically shook her head. The police and Victim Support groups had tried to put her in touch with other parents. She wanted none of it.

"We should," he said, putting his arm around her. "There'll be other people who are going through this sort of pain. Maybe we can help them."

I looked at him and my mum. His hair was long, flicking over an untidy collar. He'd sold the bakery some months before and hadn't worked since. My mum's face was the colour of wax and she had lost so much weight that the coat she was wearing swamped her shoulders. At the time I thought he really meant that: that he and my mum could help others in the same situation. Now, I think it was the other way round. It was my mum and dad who needed the help. They were the ones drifting in a boat on a flat, glassy sea, praying for a breeze to give them some direction.

So CHILDLOSS was born. My dad took control of it immediately. He linked up with the police and did the initial press briefings. He wrote an article for a national newspaper. All the while he kept explaining it to me and my mum.

"This keeps us in the public eye. It's a constant reminder to people about Judy. If she's out there this could help us find her."

My mum's mouth opened slightly at this. It was something she hadn't considered. She began to take an interest. She got her sister Rosie, and Jeff, Rosie's husband, involved. She held a meeting for other parents who had got in touch after the newspaper article. She bought a computer and she and my dad learned how to use it. They got up earlier in the mornings and when I came in from school I'd find them sitting in the middle of piles of paper. They were always on the phone to someone, talking, making arrangements.

I watched them change. My mum bought new clothes for public meetings. My dad went on a television chat show and talked about the importance of CHILDLOSS. They bought mobile phones and a fax machine. There were calendars stuck to the wall in the hallway, one for my dad and one for my mum. They each had commitments, people to see, press statements to make, television and newspaper interviews.

By the time the second anniversary came, they were like different people. They had replaced Judy with all this other stuff. We still walked along Willow Drive and placed flowers on the tree, but this time we had reporters with us. I left my mum talking to someone from a Sunday newspaper, and walked off with my dad and a pile of leaflets we were going to deliver. *Just to jog people's memories*, my dad said. There was the photo of Judy and the words WE'RE STILL MISSING JUDY at the top. At the bottom was the CHILDLOSS logo: a matchstick child drawn inside the belly of a question mark.

I finished my side of the street first and I wandered over to Sparrow Gardens, a small park that Judy and I had gone to a number of times. I leaned on the railings and looked in at the swings and the roundabout and the old-fashioned climbing frame. I was feeling depressed, I admit. Being in Willow Drive always made me feel uneasy, as though I was walking back in time. I wasn't really focusing on the children in the park but a sudden flash of pink caught my eye as it moved back and forth across my vision. My breath caught in my throat for a few moments until I looked at the swings and saw Judy there. I saw her face and her curly hair, coming towards me and then receding back out of sight, her feet kicking upwards to propel the swing. It went higher and higher and I only caught glimpses of her. My sister. My legs went weak. When the swing began to slow down I felt myself moving towards her. I couldn't stop myself. I put my arm up to wave but she didn't notice; and when she finally got off the swing another child, much older, a teenager, pulled her along out of the tiny park. I couldn't let her just disappear. I followed, I shouted. When I got closer I screamed for her to stop but the two of them just rushed on. I was quicker on my feet, though, and I outran them and grabbed the small girl, holding on to her. *Judy*, I sobbed, *I've found you*.

Then my dad was there disentangling me from the little girl, apologizing to the teenager. A woman was running towards us in the distance and I could see her face twisted up in rage. My dad turned and looked unhappily towards the street where we had come from, at a couple of police officers who were walking by.

It was the first of many times when I thought I'd seen Judy.

"Are you with us, Kim?"

I heard my teacher's voice and realized where I was. Sitting in a classroom in front of a table that was covered in slippery leaflets. The other groups had finished their tasks. The two girls on my table were talking quietly together and the boy was looking fed-up.

I felt breathless as though I'd just run some distance. The teacher had a concerned expression on her face. The others were all looking round at me. I picked up a few of the leaflets. How stupid. I'd let myself down again. I'd promised Pam I would stop revisiting the past.

"Sorry," I said, "I was day-dreaming."

After the lesson I walked towards the canteen. A girl I knew stopped me and said, "Tessa Russell is looking for you. Says she's got something really important to tell you."

I saw her across the canteen, sitting on her boyfriend's knee, surrounded by a gaggle of friends. She had a short skirt on and heavy sparkly boots. She was talking into a mobile phone and hadn't seen me. I decided to skip lunch and headed off in the direction of the library.

She was the last person I felt like talking to.

# SIX

Pam's office was like a sauna. I had to take off my jumper and open the top buttons of my blouse. Pam had gone out to speak with one of the secretaries and I pulled my mobile phone out of my bag to switch it off. The envelope icon was on the screen. I opened up the text message. MUST SPEAK WITH YOU URGENTLY. TESSA.

I groaned. For three days in a row Teresa Russell had tried to corner me. She'd left messages with my mum, my tutor and Clare. She'd also sent text messages. I would have to talk to her, just to get her to lay off.

Pam came back in. She was carrying a couple of mugs of tea.

We sat in armchairs opposite each other. In-between us was a small round coffee table on which there was a jug of water and a glass and a box of tissues. Pam had her hair tied back and no make-up. She was wearing her usual trousers and blouse. It was a sort of uniform she always had on in the office. I'd run into her in a shopping centre one day, and she'd been wearing flowery, floaty clothes with masses of jewellery and her hair hanging round her face. I almost hadn't recognized her.

"How are your mum and dad?" she said.

"They're fine," I said.

That morning, before I'd left for Pam's session, they'd received a registered envelope from the TV company that made the programme. Inside it were five copies of computer-enhanced images of my sister, long and short hair, blonde and dark. They looked exactly like photographs, a little blurry round the edges, but the head and shoulders shot looked like a real live teenager posing for a camera. My mum laid them out on the kitchen table and examined each one carefully, moving and straightening them, feeling the paper and touching the corners. My dad stood back and looked from a distance.

Added to this, the policeman who was nominally in charge of Judy's file had rung up and told my mum that there had been thirty-two calls after the programme. Thirty-two people who thought they knew something about a missing girl from eight years before. My mum had been breathless telling us. My dad had looked downright wary.

"I saw the programme," Pam said, sitting back, holding her cup and blowing gently into it.

"Yes," was all I said.

We sat in silence for a moment. I knew that I should tell her about following the girl and being taken home by the police. It was a setback and it needed to be discussed. She wouldn't judge me for it. She would just nod her head sympathetically and from time to time say things like, *Why do you think you did that?* Or, *What made you stand for so long? What was it about the girl that*

44

*reminded you of Judy?* Then, after we'd thrashed it out, we'd work on some targets. She might give me a journal to write my everyday thoughts and experiences in (we'd done that a year or so ago) or she might suggest an avoidance activity. *Whenever you think you see Judy, go somewhere and sit down and write a letter to her. Focus on yourself. Tell her about your life since you last saw her.*

In all these sessions we never mentioned *death* or *murder*. These words were buried under a landslide of soothing talk. It wasn't Pam's fault. It was her job. But I was getting weary of it all.

"I want to talk about Teresa Russell," I said suddenly, surprising myself.

"OK," Pam said, nodding her head wisely.

"She keeps bothering me, sending me phone messages. I wish she'd just leave me alone."

"You were good friends once."

"When we were kids."

"Until Judy disappeared?" Pam asked, the word *disappeared* said quietly.

I nodded, slightly cross with myself for bringing it up. What was the point? I knew why I'd stopped wanting to be with Teresa Russell.

"Tell me about the things you used to do together. When you were first friends. How did you meet, for example?"

I shrugged my shoulders. Walking down memory lane wasn't exactly what I'd had in mind for today's session. But then, I had no idea what else I wanted to talk about, so I started to tell Pam about me and Teresa Russell.

We weren't particular friends in school, although we were in the same class. We were both reluctant attendees at a summer activity club which was held at the local leisure centre. After a week of dragging ourselves through swimming, canoeing, climbing, playing football and rounders, we became close, walking home together, meeting up in the morning on the way there. We were eight years old and interested in the same things, books, writing stories, collecting magazines. We fancied ourselves as clothes designers and had sketchbooks full of ideas for jeans, tops, dresses, coats, shoes. Teresa had even sent some of hers off to a proper fashion house, and she'd got a letter back thanking her and praising some *very original ideas*.

For this reason (and no other) we collected dolls' clothes. She had several Barbie-type dolls and masses of outfits that they wore. Sometimes her mum helped us to make things for them and we had fashion shows. My Aunt Rosie liked to browse in charity shops, so she often picked up secondhand dolls' clothes and we added them to our collection. These had to be hidden from Judy who just wanted to play with them. For us (we were clear on this) it wasn't a game. It was a serious artistic pursuit.

I envied Teresa's lifestyle. Her house was always spic and span, the beds made, the carpets vacuumed. Her mum had been a machinist in a clothes factory but had given her job up when Teresa arrived. She seemed to spend most of her days doing things for her daughter. She had a giant sewing machine in her spare room and made Teresa every item of clothing that it was possible to make. She only had to look at something in a magazine or a shop window and she could reproduce it. When she wasn't doing that she was baking: cakes, bread, muffins, tarts. I loved looking at all the equipment she had: the bowls and trays, the moulds, the tiny paper cups with the pleated edges. Teresa's house always seemed to have a sweet, warm smell about it. Unlike ours, which always seemed to smell of Toby.

When Judy started school it affected our friendship. My mum mostly picked her up at the end of the day, but when she couldn't I had to collect her from the reception class and she came home with Teresa and me. She usually talked the whole way.

"What happens to all the leaves when they fall off the trees?"

"Look at that silly yellow car!"

"Why is that house painted blue?"

We largely ignored her, walking closely together, whispering about our latest plan. That was what it was like that last Friday when Teresa asked me to go round her house the next afternoon. We were going to use her new jewellery set to design and make some bracelets and necklaces. Judy skirted around us, catching odd words.

"What jewellery?"

Teresa tutted at her and I didn't answer. It wasn't any of her business. She was a gooseberry and it annoyed me having to look after her.

When my mum dropped me and Judy off at Teresa's house the next day the first thing she wanted to do was to play with the dolls and their clothes. Teresa was in a mood and wasn't even cheered up by the five pounds.

"So it wasn't a good afternoon?" Pam said.

I shook my head.

"Does that make you feel unhappy? That the last hours you spent with Judy were bad?"

"Yes, I guess so…"

A beeping sound startled me. It was like a mobile phone but it wasn't my ring tone, and anyway I knew that I had turned mine off. Pam started to pat at her waist.

"I'm really sorry, Kim. It's my beeper. I wouldn't answer it, only it's an emergency call. Will you just give me five minutes?"

I nodded and she left the room, tutting to herself. The office door banged and I found myself feeling agitated. I remembered then that Teresa Russell had had a cardboard box in her bedroom full of remnants of fabric. These were left-over bits from clothes or curtains that Mrs Russell had made. There were dozens of them. We often spent hours cutting designs from them and sewing them up on to our models. That afternoon Judy had desperately wanted to play with them but Teresa wouldn't let her.

"We're not designing clothes today, we're making jewellery," she said firmly, getting her equipment out and laying it on the table.

"Can I make a necklace?" Judy asked, edging up to us.

"You can't play with this!" Teresa snapped. "It's full of tiny bits. You might swallow one!"

"What would happen, Kim, if I swallowed a bead?"

"You'd die a slow and agonizing death," Teresa said, before I could speak.

Judy looked at me, but I turned away exasperated. Teresa tutted loudly and went back to her jewellery kit. After a while I heard little sobs and glanced round to see Judy shuddering, her face the colour of beetroot. When she started to cry more loudly Teresa realized she had gone too far.

"Sssh," she said, looking at her bedroom door, afraid that her mum might hear. She put her arm round Judy's shoulder and led her over to the bed, "You sit down and be a good girl and Kim and I will play a special game with you."

Judy put her thumb in her mouth and sat on the bed. Teresa and I continued making our necklaces. If Judy had been able to sit quietly for a while maybe things would have been all right. She couldn't, though. She had to talk. We ignored most of her chatter and just let it ride over us but every now and then she insisted on an answer. I made a lot of *ums* but Teresa was irritated by her, I could tell.

"When are we going to play that special game?" she'd said, her voice beginning to sound whiny.

Teresa was having trouble with the necklace she was making – the wire had become tangled and she was getting cross. When Judy asked again about the special game Teresa lost her temper and threw the half-finished necklace across the table so that dozens of beads bounced off it and scattered on to the floor.

"Oh," Judy said. "Will your mum tell you off?"

Teresa took a deep breath and folded her arms.

"Our special game," she said, darkly, "is hide and seek."

Judy jumped up, happy. It was a game she played with Dad and me. She loved it. I looked at my friend, amazed at the change. Perhaps she was going to let Judy join in after all.

I was wrong. Teresa had other plans. She said that I was "it". I had to close my eyes and count to one hundred, and she and Judy were going to hide. I heard them getting further away from me and I was up to sixty-odd when I felt a hand on my shoulder. It was Teresa and she was gleeful.

"I've hidden Judy in the laundry cupboard. Now we can get some peace."

I looked in the direction of the hallway. Judy would be curled up among the towels and sheets, bristling with excitement about being found. But Teresa planned to just leave her there.

I should have stopped her. I should have insisted that

Judy be allowed to play with us or with the dolls and their clothes. Who wouldn't have? She was my sister. I shouldn't have let Teresa treat her like that. But I said nothing and we continued with the jewellery. It was twenty minutes before Judy crept into the room, her face crimson with the heat of the cupboard. When she saw us sitting at the table she knew she had been fooled. She didn't speak but went and lay on the bed. I felt uneasy and kept looking at her out of the corner of my eye. She had started the afternoon like a bright, playful puppy and now she was miserable, looking round at us periodically with reproachful eyes. Teresa's mood had brightened and she started to hum a song. On the table were two finished necklaces. Hers was the nicest one. Mine looked misshapen and tatty. I didn't want to play any more, so I suggested that we went out to the shop to spend the five-pound note. Judy looked tired, as if she'd rather not come, but I persuaded her. "I'll buy you something nice," I said.

It was the one act of kindness we had shown her all afternoon.

"Sorry, Kim. That was one of my clients who's having real problems at the moment. I had to speak to her." Pam bustled in, the open door creating a welcome breeze in the hot room. She sat down again and looked expectantly at me.

"We were talking about Teresa and you," she said, "and that last afternoon."

"Yes," I said, my fingers tapping the arms of the chair. "It wasn't a good afternoon."

I felt curiously close to tears. This was strange. It had been a long time since I'd cried for Judy, years perhaps. Pam sat up straight, businesslike. I could see she was thinking, composing some response.

"Many bereaved people feel guilt about the last hours they spent with their loved ones. They always wish that they'd acted differently, been more loving, more caring. A wife has a row with her husband at breakfast and then he is hit and killed by a bus. Even though they were a happy, loving couple, she will always have that terrible sense of guilt that they parted on a bad note. Sudden, unexpected loss doesn't give people a chance to end things as they would want."

I nodded tightly.

"You can't let those last few difficult hours you spent with Judy spoil the rest of your memories. She was your sister and you had her for five years. That's what you must think about, not the last afternoon."

"I do," I said.

"And Teresa Russell?"

"We stopped being friends a long time ago," I said.

"That's OK. Everyone moves on, makes new friends," Pam said, glancing at her watch.

I nodded to please her. But it wasn't as simple as that. It wasn't that I'd *moved on*. Once my sister had gone I could no longer stand to be in the company of Teresa Russell. For a long time I couldn't even bear to look at her.

# SEVEN

When I got home I found my house unexpectedly full of people. As the front door opened, I heard the buzz of conversation coming from the living room. I was surprised. It was three-thirty on a Tuesday afternoon, not the usual time for a meeting of any sort. I opened the living-room door and the conversation came to a halt. My mum stood up from among a group of people and came across to me.

"Kim," she said, grabbing my hand. "We've heard some news."

I looked around. My dad was leaning against the wall near the window. He looked edgy. My Aunt Rosie was fiddling with a bouquet of flowers that were in a glass vase on the coffee table. A woman from the support group was sitting with a smile on her face. Two police officers were there as well, the plain-clothes one that had been dealing with the case for the past couple of years and a young woman in uniform.

"What?" I said, puzzled.

"Sit down, sit down," my mum said excitedly.

I was puzzled. There was a festive atmosphere in the room. I half expected to look up and see bunting strung from one corner to the other.

"Hello, Kim."

It was the WPC. I recognized her then. She was the officer who had picked me up from outside the small girl's house the previous week. The day of the TV programme.

"Why don't *you* tell her," my mum said to the plain-clothes policeman, Detective Inspector Robinson or Robbins or Roberts. I could never remember which.

I sat down and my Aunt Rosie bustled over and sat next to me. For once she had no knitting, and I noticed how she wove her fingers in and out of each other. The policeman pulled over a chair from the dining table and set it down in front of me. He was wearing a dark suit, the jacket just a little too tight. As he sat down he pulled up the knees of his trousers. I looked down at his feet and saw that his black socks had Homer Simpson on each ankle. Part of me wanted to laugh.

"After the television programme we got a number of calls from members of the public. Your mum's probably already told you that."

I nodded.

"We follow them all up, of course, but after eight years we don't really expect much. They're usually well-meaning people who want to help. Something on the programme triggers a memory, but ninety-nine times out of a hundred it's a false one."

I knew this. It happened after the early TV programmes. There had been excitement when we found out how many people had phoned in, but it had always ended up coming to nothing.

"Yesterday we went to a house in Willow Drive. The

people who live there only moved in three months ago. They've been doing some building work and that kind of stuff."

"Overhauling the gardens," my mum interrupted.

"Yes. The front garden was one of those paved affairs. Crazy paving."

"Very unfashionable nowadays," Rosie said. "We never get any call for crazy paving."

"And when the builders tore it up," my mum added, "they found Judy's pink top."

"What?" I said.

"We don't know that it's Judy's," the WPC interrupted. "We can't be sure of that until the forensic people look at it. Until you have a chance to look at it yourself."

The pink top. Judy's special fleece that had been bought the week before she disappeared. It had been in a garden in Willow Drive, only metres from where I last saw her.

"I don't understand," I said.

I wasn't being dim. The people along Willow Drive had been interviewed, the gardens searched for clues. Why hadn't something been picked up? Found at the time?

"The present owners uncovered the top about ten days ago. They stuck it in a rubbish bag but when they saw the programme they got it out again. If it turns out to be Judy's then we will apply for permission for a further search."

"It's an important clue," my mum said.

I looked at my dad who gave a little shrug of his shoulders.

"Why wasn't it found at the time?" I demanded.

People started to look puzzled. They could see that I wasn't as thrilled with the information as my mum.

"Our officers did do a preliminary search of the area," the inspector said.

"And we don't know for sure yet if it is Judy's top," the WPC said again.

"Look, Kim," the inspector said, his voice softening. "A missing child investigation is probably the most high profile of all police work that there is. We put every officer on to it that we can spare. In the end, though, decisions have to be made. We simply cannot scour every square centimetre of ground. We did a lot of searches in that first week, but then the focus of the investigation changed. Once we knew about the red van we put our resources into trying to find it."

The red van.

I made myself look away from him, my eyes travelling down to the socks, black with the yellow figure of Homer Simpson on each side. This time it didn't make me want to laugh. I felt angry. I felt like reaching down and pulling the cartoon character off and tearing it to pieces.

The red van had taken up all the manpower. I knew that. For weeks they'd scoured the country for a van with X and P in the registration number. They found quite a few, interviewed the owners, checked out alibis. One man had even been arrested and held for questioning for over twenty-four hours. I knew it all. I looked down at my lap and saw that my hands had turned into tiny hard fists.

"I don't think Kim's feeling very well," my dad said.

"We should be going anyway," the inspector said, standing up, his trousers dropping over the offending socks. "We'll see you and your wife down at the station in the morning. About ten?"

They left quietly, a lot of mumbling words coming from out in the hall. I felt Rosie's arm around me, her perfume strong and sweet.

"We all know how you feel," she said. "But this is good. This could be the beginning of the end. We might find out what happened to Judy now. That's what's important."

I nodded silently. She meant that we might find Judy's body. The pink top might not be the only thing buried in the gardens in Willow Drive. Then we could have a funeral with flowers and a black car.

"You and your mum and dad could look ahead. You could start afresh."

Her arm was tightly clasped around my shoulders, her voice lowered to a whisper. I felt trapped on the seat and didn't have the strength to shake her off. My mum came back into the room then, looking happier than I'd seen her for a long time.

"Cup of tea?" my dad said and went out to the kitchen.

"This is good," my mum said. "This is closure."

*Closure.* That horrible American word. I shook off my aunt's arm and stood up. I left them in the living room, picked up my jacket from the hall and went out of the front door. I could hear my mum coming after me but I quickened my pace and was turning out of the garden before she managed to open the front door. It was bitterly cold outside, the wind like a razor on my face. I glanced back and saw her standing in the doorway. She didn't call out, so I put my head down and walked along the street, not really sure of where I was going. I just knew I didn't want to sit there and listen to everyone's delight about the possibility of finding my sister's body. Who would?

It was dusk and some car headlights were on and some weren't. There was a hint of dampness in the chill wind and I pulled the edges of my jacket close around my neck. A feeling of gloom was swirling round me, making the air seem thick and dark so that each footstep was heavier than the last. From behind I heard a car horn beeping. I hoped it wasn't my mum or dad. I walked on, my feet feeling like lead weights, not really looking where I was going. I was just about to cross a road when a car pulled round the corner and stopped directly in front of me. The passenger door swung open and the interior light snapped on, making the car look warm and inviting against the navy-blue sky.

"Kim, I've been trying to get hold of you for days," a bright voice said.

I saw Teresa Russell in the passenger seat. She was half leaning out of the car. In the driver's seat was the boyfriend, Danny. She smiled up at me, oblivious to the fact that I wasn't delighted to see her.

"I need to talk to you," she said excitedly. "I've got something important to tell you. Get in."

She reached behind and opened the rear door. I stepped back. I was not in the mood to swap college gossip with her or find out about her course or boyfriend or her wonderful life. I'd made it quite clear that I wasn't interested in associating with her at all. I began to shake my head.

"Listen, Kim. This is important. Really important. It's about your sister, Judy. I can't tell you here, you need to come back to my house."

"Judy?" I said, surprised.

"You'll want to hear it, I promise you. This is no joke. I'm deadly serious, aren't I, Dan?"

The boyfriend turned and nodded, his fingers twitching on the steering wheel. It had started to rain, icy darts that kept changing direction, hitting the skin of my face and hands. I looked around, not knowing what to do.

"Just half an hour at my place. That's all. Then Dan'll drive you home, won't you?" She turned and looked at the boyfriend again.

"Get in," he said with a wave of his arm. "I'm freezing my backside off sitting here with the doors open."

"Please," Teresa said.

I got in. She'd said it was about Judy and that was the only reason that I was willing to talk to her.

# EIGHT

Teresa's house had changed a lot over eight years. It was no longer the tidy, quiet haven it had been when she and I were best friends. When I walked in the first thing I noticed was the pushchair in the hall. Teresa saw me looking at it.

"Did you know my mum and dad split up? He lives in South London with his girlfriend, and Trevor lives here with mum. And Sarah."

She rolled her eyes pleasantly in the direction of the pushchair.

"Almost three years old. She's a real sweetie. Isn't she, Dan?"

The Boyfriend grunted. He'd screeched to a halt outside Teresa's house and parked half up on the pavement. He'd wanted to wait in the car but Teresa had insisted he came in.

Teresa's mum came into the hall. She was wearing sporty clothes and her hair was up in a ponytail. She looked taller or thinner or something. She had bright-red lipstick on. She was carrying a wriggling toddler.

"Tess," she said, breathlessly, "I'm glad you're back. I've got to take food round to the pub in about half an hour and I need you to stay with Sarah. I'll be twenty minutes tops –"

She stopped speaking abruptly, and looked quizzically in my direction. It took her a minute but then she recognized me.

"It's Kim Hockney. How lovely to see you! Come in, come in. Let me look at you!"

There was a fuss in the kitchen with Teresa's mum talking ten to the dozen. *The name's not Russell any more, call me Jo!* She made a great fuss of me. *Tea? Coffee? Soft drink? Sparkling water?* She took my jacket and held it for ages, meaning to hang it up. Finally she put it round the back of one of the chairs. She talked about my family, *Mum? Dad? I've seen them in the papers. Your mum's been absolutely brilliant, everyone says so.* All the while Teresa was sitting with Sarah on her lap, the Boyfriend leaning languidly against the worktop, having helped himself to a can of Coke from the fridge. How was I? Teresa's mum asked. How was I coping these days? Was I getting on with my life? *That's so important*, she said. *You must get on with your own life.*

She put a cup of tea in front of me, and a plate with some biscuits.

"Don't get a chance to do much home baking these days," she said, smiling.

I remembered the jam tarts. There in that very kitchen. The units and decor were different but the table was still in the same place. We'd used special trays and rubbed lumps of butter round them so that the pastry wouldn't stick. They'd overcooked, I remembered, but it hadn't mattered because nobody felt like eating them anyway.

"Mum's got her own catering business now?" Teresa said, jiggling the small girl up and down on her lap.

"With Trevor, my new husband – which reminds me, I'd better be off or else he'll give me the sack."

She picked up a giant bunch of keys from the side and bent down to kiss Sarah and then Teresa.

"Lovely to see you, Kim. You must come back and see us again."

And then she was gone. I looked from Teresa to the Boyfriend, and then at the tiny girl.

"What's this all about?" I said. "I'm supposed to be somewhere."

I glanced at my watch to make the point. I wanted to be off, to be out of that house.

"Dan, take Sarah in to watch one of her videos? I'll take Kim up to my room?"

In the short time I'd been with Teresa I noticed the way her sentences sometimes went up at the end. Even when there was no question. It was as if she wanted some kind of answer to every single thing that she said. She didn't get any from the Boyfriend. He just took an irritated breath and picked the small girl up. His mood was a bit of a front, though, because I could hear him giving the little girl a kiss and promising her some *Postman Pat*. She went with him without a backward glance and Teresa beckoned for me to follow her upstairs.

Her bedroom was a lot tidier than the rest of the house.

"Sarah doesn't come in here," she explained. "Mum's really good about that. She says I need my personal space? What with Trevor living here as well. It's not so bad. He's nice, Trevor, and he's always giving me money. My dad's the same. Who says divorce is bad for the kids?"

She was being relentlessly cheerful in the face of my disinterest.

"Why did you want to see me?" I said, being direct. "You said it was about Judy."

She plonked on to the bed and I walked around the room, looking faintly bored. The walls looked as though they'd been freshly painted and were dotted with clipframes, mostly photos of Teresa at different ages. The bed was neatly made, the duvet puffed up like a shop display. There were bookshelves on the wall that had lines of paperbacks on them. Murder mystery novels, all in alphabetical order of the writer. There was a fitted desk in the corner with a computer on it and a shelf underneath for the printer. There was a pen tidy with a variety of biros and highlighters and felt-tips. There were white plastic stacking boxes with handwritten labels. There was nothing untidy on any surface, no pages of notes, folders, sweet wrappers or ring binders.

"I've spent the last couple of months trying to be friendly with you," she said. There was the beginnings of a pout on her face.

"I'm not interested in being friends, Teresa."

"It wasn't my fault, you know. I never meant for anything bad to happen? I don't have a guilty conscience about Judy."

I looked at her with distaste. This was a conversation I didn't want to have. I had never said she was guilty of anything. To tell the absolute truth, I had never said anything to her about it. After that night I'd sunk back into my family. I'd been ill, taken months off school. When I finally returned she had other friends and we had nothing to say to each other.

"It wasn't anybody's fault. What was it you want to see me about?"

She gave a forced smile and looked as though she was thinking hard, weighing something up. After a moment she seemed to make a decision to talk.

"I wasn't sure whether or not to talk to you about this. Dan says I shouldn't. He says it might just cause trouble and unnecessary upset?"

I raised my eyebrows, wanting to smile. I couldn't imagine Dan saying anything that sounded so grown-up. Teresa swallowed and then continued speaking. I slouched back against the chest of drawers.

"I might as well start at the beginning. In August, me, Mum, Sarah and Trevor, we went to Florida. To Disneyland."

Her voice was faltering a bit. I wondered what her holiday in the sun had to do with my missing sister.

"Anyway, while we were there we met this family? Americans, they were. They came from Seattle. That's right on the north-west tip of the USA. It's almost as far from Florida as London is. There was Holly and Rob and their daughter Shelly. Apparently it's always pretty cold in Seattle, so they often go to hot places."

She was gathering speed.

"Me and Shelly, we hung around together? We got to know each other quite well. We all talked about our families and our friends and stuff. She had this great wad of photos that she carried everywhere with her and she showed me her house, her school, her mates, her boyfriend, her car..."

She shrugged her shoulders and seemed unsure about going on.

"Like I said, she had this photo album. Every time she told me about someone new she fished the album out of her bag and pointed to whoever it was. Some of the photos had been taken at this barbecue her family had had. There were loads of people round, but Shelly picked out this one woman, her next-door neighbour, and told me about her. Her name is Margaret and she has an adopted teenage daughter who originally came from England. She showed me a photo of the girl."

She was quiet. Staring at me. I couldn't quite see the point.

"The daughter's name is Judy."

She gave me a steady look. I wasn't sure what to make of it. It was as if she'd said something really significant and I'd missed it. The next-door neighbour's adopted child's name was Judy. So what?

"Margaret, the neighbour, moved next door to them about five years ago. She'd been travelling round Europe for a couple of years and had adopted an English girl whose family had been killed in a car crash. The girl's thirteen now and her name is Judy."

I saw the point suddenly. I almost laughed.

"Wait a minute. Are you saying what I think you're saying? That this woman took my sister to America with her? Don't be ridiculous."

"Wait," she said. "Wait, I've not finished yet."

She got up and went across to her computer, switching it on. I watched her while a feeling of indignation was building up in my chest. How could she suggest such a story to me? Did she have any idea how upsetting it was? She was sitting down, fiddling with her mouse, and the computer was building itself up, throwing icons on to the screen, making beeping noises. I noticed her clicking on *My Documents* and I waited to see what she would say next.

"At the time, when we were in Disneyland? Shelly mentioned this woman and her daughter, saying how the kid had an English background but spoke with an American accent. Anyway, her mum overheard us and she told this story about Margaret's background. Apparently Shelly didn't even know it. It seems that Margaret had had a four-year-old daughter of her own who had died in a swimming pool accident. That's when she'd gone travelling round Europe. Trying to get over it."

She looked expectantly at me. She'd clicked on to a document and opened it up. It was a page of print and looked like an email that had been saved.

"At the time, I didn't think much of it? You know, it twigged with me, a bit strange. This woman adopting a kid in England. I mean you hear about people going to eastern European countries to adopt, or China or somewhere, but England? The fact that she was called Judy didn't really register at the time. It's not what you'd call a common name, but it's not unusual either. When I first heard about the kid I did think about your Judy, but only because it was the same name."

"It's a coincidence."

"I know it is. And if that's all it was then I wouldn't have said anything. But when I got back and started college one of the first people I bumped into was you. It brought it all back to me. It made me think about what happened all those years ago. Because it was on my mind I emailed Shelly about it."

She was quiet, expecting me to say something.

"She emailed me right back the very same day and she said, *Wouldn't it be amazing if your friend's sister and my next-door neighbour were the same girl!*"

"That's ridiculous!" I said.

"We chatted about it for a few days. Shelly even emailed me a couple of pictures of the girl for *identification*, but we weren't really serious. We were just messing around. We went on to other things and I forgot about it until the TV programme. When they showed that computer picture of your sister? I thought it looked familiar, as if I'd seen the kid somewhere. It nagged at me for a few minutes and then I remembered. I went straight up to the computer and looked up the photo."

Teresa fiddled with the mouse and then there was a picture on the screen. It was a group photograph. People in shorts mostly, all standing round a barbecue.

"Come and look."

I went closer, pushing down a feeling of impatience.

"That's Shelly and her mum. And that's Margaret, the next-door neighbour."

They were suntanned types, in shorts and dark glasses. The teenage girl was waving at the camera, the woman was holding a plate with food on. The neighbour looked different. She was wearing a dress that almost came down to her ankles. She was plump with hamster cheeks.

"This is Judy."

Teresa pointed to a smaller girl on the left of the picture. She was wearing cut-off jeans and a strappy T-shirt. Beside the others she looked very pale. She had a banana grin on her face and was holding one of those giant paper cups with a straw out of the top. She looked ordinary enough. She did have tight curly hair, though, and her skin was almost white.

"She could be anyone," I said, narrowing my eyes to get a clearer look.

"But look at this other picture. It's a close-up."

She clicked and another photo appeared. A head and shoulders shot, taken perhaps a few minutes later. The girl still had the giant cup of drink in her hand. There was something about her, though I couldn't put my finger on it. Teresa opened a drawer and pulled out a newspaper cutting. It was a small copy of the image that had been used on the LOST CHILDREN programme. She held it up to the screen. Both photos were a bit blurry, but in spite of my irritation I did look closely. There was a kind of similarity between the two pictures.

"See?" Teresa said, looking earnestly at me.

Then my eye caught something in the American photograph. Around the girl's neck was a chain, and hanging from it, just visible below the paper cup, was a "J". I didn't speak. I remembered Judy's necklace. The one she kept putting in her mouth. *Don't suck that*, my mum was always saying, *it's covered in germs*.

"Don't they look alike?" Teresa said.

I nodded.

"That's what I thought! I said to Shelly, *What if it is her?* What if this woman snatched her off the street, hid her and then, when all the fuss had died down, took her to America?"

Teresa's voice had a dramatic edge to it. She emphasized the word *snatched* as if she was reading a play script. It irritated me. I looked away and found my eyes resting on her shelf of books – murder mysteries, one after the other. She spent a lot of her time reading them. That's what this was to her. A murder mystery, and she was trying to solve it. I didn't like it.

"How could someone snatch a five-year-old girl and take her to America? There were police at the airports!" I said.

"Only for the first few days. And don't forget they were probably looking for a *man*. Not a woman."

"How would she get her to America? What about a passport?"

"But that's the clever bit? She probably did have a passport. An American one; for her own dead daughter."

I stood up straight. I didn't like this. Not at all. If it had been complete nonsense I would have just shrugged it off. Instead I found myself drawn to the computer screen, to the teenager with the giant cardboard cup of drink and the gold "J" hanging round her neck. For a second I had a desperate need to know what she was like. I wondered about her height, her voice, her teeth and her favourite clothes. My sister Judy, grown-up. There was this tiny bubble of hope inside my chest, and I wanted to go away and be on my own to think about it.

Teresa was looking at me expectantly. From downstairs I could hear the squeal of a child's voice involved in some game or other. It was a sound of pure delight, and yet it grated on me. This whole thing, this holiday story, was extremely unlikely. In my head I knew it. It was some American girl, and not my sister at all. I shrank back, feeling foolish. I must have looked upset because Teresa stood up. She put her hand out to me but I didn't take it.

"I can't … I don't want to talk about…"

"I understand."

"No," I whispered. "You don't understand."

"I do," she said. "Especially since Sarah—"

"NO, YOU DON'T!"

She stepped back, affronted. Her expression of sympathy wavered, and underneath I thought I saw a hint of truculence. She was annoyed because I hadn't been bowled over by her theory. I walked out of her room and quickly down the stairs. The Boyfriend was standing at the bottom, holding the toddler in his arms.

"I said it was a silly idea," he said. "I told her it was all rubbish."

I ignored him and went out into the street.

# NINE

I found myself walking along Willow Drive. It was raining, the wind blowing the spray in different directions. I pulled my collar up round my neck, keeping the cold from my skin. My hair and face were getting wet, but I didn't care. It was refreshing after the heat of Teresa Russell's house.

Willow Drive was a long road that cut across six or seven streets of suburban housing. There were no corner shops or pubs, just road after road of tastefully-built brick houses, their gardens overflowing into the streets. The pavements were lined with trees and the parked cars sat on either side of the road. It was a quiet area. There were very few people around. That's why the houses were sought after. You could walk along this street, from one end to the other, and only pass by a couple of people.

*Weeping Willow Drive*, one of the newspapers had called it. The street where Judy vanished. Nobody saw anything. Nobody was expecting a five-year-old girl to be walking out alone in the dark. I was the only one who knew she was there. I let her stomp off, thinking she would turn round and come back when her temper had waned.

Someone else had seen her, though. We all knew that,

even if we didn't say it. My sister didn't simply fade into the mists; she wasn't sucked up by extra-terrestrials; she didn't slip between the rungs of a drain. Someone – most definitely a man – saw her and took her away. It was as simple as that.

Part of me had realized this during those first few days. It was an unspoken thing, but it hung in the air of our living room like a black cloud. It was in my mum and dad's eyes and on the tips of their tongues. It weighed down every glance between Beth and Rob, the police officers. Everyday sounds, the front door bell and the phone ringing, these things became heavy with menace.

When they showed me the book of men's photographs it became certain in my mind. Then I said I'd seen the red van, and it seemed to fit so perfectly with what the police wanted. There had to be a vehicle, how else could a small child be snatched up and ferried away? The police had fallen hungrily on my clue. Why not a van? Just open the back doors and bundle her in. Perhaps he knocked her out first. Perhaps he just stuffed something in her mouth and said, *Be a good girl and I won't hurt you.*

I stood still for a minute, the rain falling in front of me, only visible in the yellow streetlights, a thin curtain of water. My breaths had shortened and I didn't feel that I could take another step. In front of me there was only wet pavement, but it looked different, like the surface of some dark, oily pool, and I couldn't bring myself to put my foot on to it. Neither could I turn round. I was stuck, and from somewhere deep down I felt this panic in my ribs like some struggling animal.

This was not good. I took long deep breaths. I made myself count up to twenty. I stretched my arms out in front of me as though I was doing some odd exercise. I had to stop. I could not afford to let myself think over what might have happened to Judy. That was a dark cave into which I would not go. Pam had warned me to step back, to turn away. *Don't think it, Kim*, she said. *Nobody knows what happened to Judy*.

"Are you all right?"

A voice from behind made me jump. I turned around and saw a woman walking to her car. In her hands she had a small dog which was looking curiously at me.

"Fine," I said, in a forced voice. "Just wish I'd brought an umbrella."

I walked on, my head down. Now and then I looked up to make sure I wasn't going to walk into anything. I forced myself to think about Judy when she was still with us, and I remembered her on the day we'd got Toby.

It had been my dad's birthday, a sunny day in July when the garden seemed full of people, my mum and dad's friends, Jeff and Rosie, me and Judy. There was a barbecue, I remembered, and Dad's eyes had been watering with the smoke but he'd insisted on continuing to cook. *It's a man's job*, he'd insisted. *Men cook at barbecues. It's our caveman instinct*. My mum had given him a *don't be ridiculous* look. Judy was only two or three, a tiny bundle of mischief who had to be watched all the time. The front doorbell rang while we were all eating.

"This is Dad's birthday present!" my mum had whispered, excitedly.

She left us out in the garden, my dad with his tongs and his spatula, the rest of us sitting on chairs waiting for our food. My uncle was holding Judy on his knee, reading her a story. Every now and then she kept asking him if she could have a drink of his whisky and he laughed, holding it away from her in mid-air.

A puppy dog ran out of the back doors, its tail swishing from one side to another. It ran to the far end of the grass and then back up again, weaving in between the people who were sitting or standing. Judy struggled off my uncle's knee and ran after it. My dad stood gaping.

"What do you think?" my mum said, giving him a hug.

He was delighted, I could tell, and would have said something if the dog had not shot past Judy at that point, throwing her back into some rose bushes. She let out a scream and several people rushed over to her. The thorns had scratched her skin and there were thin red tramlines down her arms. She had to be held and petted the whole afternoon and it was days before she went near Toby.

I smiled at the memory. That was Judy. She always seemed to take centre stage at every family occasion. I glanced up and noticed some unusual lights further up the street. Looking through the rain I could make out a couple of parked police cars, although their flashing lights were not on. As I got closer I could see that there was a white tarpaulin tent over the front garden and some bright lighting inside it. Then I remembered.

Judy's pink top had been discovered underneath the crazy paving in one of the front gardens along Willow Drive. How could that have slipped my mind? I walked on and drew level with the police cars. There was a single officer sitting in the passenger seat of one of them. The car's sidelights were on and from time to time the windscreen wiper cleared away the rain and he looked out at me.

I must have seemed an odd figure, standing out in the downpour. He made a hand signal for me to go away. I didn't, though. I stood looking at the front garden covered with a flimsy tent. There was movement inside it, one or two figures, perhaps. I wondered if they were still digging, like archaeologists, trying to recreate the past. The door of the police car clicked open. I turned away from the garden and began to walk back home.

Wasn't that what we'd all been doing these last eight years? Trying to put the fragments of that day back together? Even Teresa Russell had tried. I thought about her American woman. She was dark, I remembered, with plump cheeks. What had Teresa thought? That this woman had been walking or driving along Willow Drive and seen a little five-year-old girl appear out of the darkness? I shook my head. That she'd come to this area and *by chance* found a child? I didn't believe it. Who would?

Walking towards my own front door I noticed how very wet I was. The rain was running off my jacket and my hair was flattened down to my head. The door sprang open before I got a chance to knock.

"Kim! Where did you go? I was so worried."

My mum was standing on the step and she pulled me into the hallway.

"You're soaked. What have you been doing?"

"I just went for a walk," I said, not wanting to go into detail.

She peeled my coat off me and called for my dad and a towel. Twenty minutes later I was sitting in the bright living room, my hair hanging damply around my face, a large towelling dressing gown covering me from head to toe. In my hand was a plate with a single piece of toast on it. I took small half-moon bites from it. Everyone had gone home and the room looked strangely empty. It was an odd sight; there was usually someone or other there to see my mum, often it was just Rosie.

The towelling gown was comfortable against my skin and the toast was buttery. I hadn't realized that I was hungry. My mum and dad were sitting side by side, both looking at me. I noticed my mum had her hand on my dad's leg, rubbing it gently.

I felt happy to be there. In that room, out of the rain, away from the house on Willow Drive, away from Teresa Russell and her extraordinary idea. I felt as if I could sink back into the chair and close my eyes and go to sleep, my mum and dad watching over me. My whole body seemed heavy and relaxed.

"We've just had Inspector Robbins on the phone with some exciting news," my mum said.

I looked up, my feeling of euphoria disintegrating.

"They've found out about the people who lived in the house on Willow Drive eight years ago. It was owned by an old woman who had to go into nursing care. Her son rented it out to people to help pay for her nursing fees. At the time when Judy went missing, it was on a six-month lease. The couple who rented it left a month or so after."

My mum was businesslike, relaying the story with absolute accuracy, I was sure. I nodded, trying to look interested. Should I have been pleased?

"The neighbours said that the garden was paved during that time. Course, the old lady is long dead and her son lives abroad. The police are trying to get in touch with him to find out who it was who rented the house for that six-month period."

"You don't know who they are then," I said, pulling the dressing gown round me, tying the belt as tightly as I could.

"No," my dad said. "All we know about them is that the woman was an American and that she went travelling around Europe afterwards. We don't know about the man."

"But the police will find out," my mum said.

An American woman. I almost laughed.

# TEN

I held back from calling Teresa Russell for two days. To tell the absolute truth I wasn't able to call anyone. I told my mum I had my period and felt unwell. I stayed at home, mostly in my room. She and my dad hardly noticed. They went to the police station and identified the pink fleece top. It was Judy's, they were sure. The police warned them not to put too much hope in it, though. The top was one of thousands that had been made for a chain store. I was sure that they were ignoring the advice because I heard their voices bubbling away downstairs, talking about Judy.

On Friday morning, when I woke up, the upset and confusion that Teresa's news had started was still lying heavily on me. I had tried to tell myself that it was just a set of coincidences, a story written on tissue paper, ready to fall apart as soon as anyone turned the pages. But I kept remembering the American girl's neck chain and the gold "J" that hung down from it. Judy had been wearing hers on the day she'd gone missing. It was many years since I'd seen it and it had startled me. It had been rather long for Judy's tiny neck and she was always fiddling with the letter, often poking it into her mouth or holding it straight out to look at it. Seeing it there, in that photograph, had been like a sign, a signal even. My sister, alive and living in another country. A tiny part of me wanted so much to believe it. Why not?

Teresa's mobile was switched off so I left her a message. It was curt.

"It's Kim here. Please bring all the stuff you have about the American girl. I need to look over it again. I'll be in college after ten."

Then I got dressed and gathered my things together. I called Clare and asked her to drop by and give me a lift. I heard her horn beeping about twenty minutes later and I walked up to the front door. I opened my mouth to say goodbye. I could hear my mum's voice from the back kitchen. She was speaking to someone on the phone. From upstairs I could hear the printer whirring. My dad. Probably printing off the CHILDLOSS newsletter. I went out of the door without a word.

"You feeling better?" Clare said, when I got in the car.

I nodded. She crunched the gears as she pulled out on to the road. There was a strong smell in the car, a bit like white spirit. I noticed a large grubby bag in the back seat that looked like it was full of her weekend washing. She saw me looking.

"Some stuff for a Still Life option I'm doing."

Her voice was a bit croaky and it was then that I saw her face looked red.

"Is everything all right?" I said, feeling immediately guilty. I was so wound up in my own problems that I hardly noticed anyone else.

"Mum's in a state. My dad wants her to sell the house.

He wants money. Freddie say she doesn't have to sell it until I finish my education. But my dad's broke." She shrugged.

Freddie was her mum's boyfriend, the computer man. I didn't know what to say. It probably suited him to be living in her mum's house. Clare's dad, on the other hand, was in rented rooms and was working all the hours he could. It was an unsolvable mess. I looked round at the still life. I could imagine an untidy pile of domestic things, shoes, brushes, ornaments, packets of cornflakes – all painted at odd angles. Knowing Clare, she would alter the perspective, making some look big and threatening and others look small and insubstantial.

It was beyond me.

"You're lucky. Your mum and dad are still together."

If anyone else had said that I would have been offended. *Lucky* was not a word that came to mind when I thought of my own family. But I knew what she meant. My mum and dad were close, there was no denying it. In the years after Judy it had been grief that had held them together, then they'd both built up the support group. Even though my mum had taken it over and my dad now played a very back-seat role there was still a powerful bond between them.

"These things usually do work out in the long run," I said, realizing how paltry the words seemed.

Clare gave a little nod and smiled. When we got to college I helped her up to the art department with her still life objects and then I went to look for Teresa

Russell. I found her at once in the canteen. Unusually, she was on her own. At her feet were a hold-all and a matching rucksack.

"Hi," she said, looking at me unsurely.

"I'm sorry I shouted at you the other day. I was a bit upset."

"That's all right. I understand. It must have been a bit of a shock?"

"Are you going away somewhere?" I said, wanting to change the subject.

"A team-building weekend. It's part of my Business Studies course. You know, rock climbing, abseiling, potholing. Dan's really jealous. He thinks I might fall for one of the instructors?" She hunched her shoulders up at the delight of it.

"Did you bring the things?" I said, keeping my voice light.

"Here. All sorted out." She pulled out a plastic folder from her rucksack. "Photographs and emails. Oh, and there's another email. Shelly sent it last night but I don't suppose it matters now."

"How do you mean?"

"Mum told me about the police finding Judy's top buried in the garden on Willow Drive. I guess that puts paid to my American theories."

I smiled noncommittally. I took the envelope of stuff and felt an urge to unpack it right there and then.

"It'll probably sort the mystery out. If they find more ... stuff," Teresa went on, her eyes avoiding mine and looking round the canteen.

"Probably," I said.

She'd finished with it. For a few days she'd been enthusiastic about the idea, like a fisherman trying to reel in a big fish. But my reaction and the news about the pink top had sapped her energy and she'd let it go, wriggling and splashing away. Her big idea.

The noise of chatter from behind me made her stand up. A couple of girls and a boy had come in, carrying bags and rucksacks. Her face broke into a smile and she thrust her chest forward.

"I must go," she said. "Email Shelly, if you want? She's really nice."

She virtually skipped across the canteen floor to where her friends were standing. I fingered the packet of stuff she'd given me. I was desperate to look at it for myself. I made my way to the library and found a study table in a corner away from most other students. Then I laid it all on the table.

There were printed copies of the emailed photographs. They were black and white and looked grainy. The sharpness of the originals had been lost. I held the small newspaper picture up beside the head and shoulders shot of the American girl. There was a resemblance but it was hard to be certain of anything. I looked at a couple of Teresa and Shelley's emails. The pair of them had got carried away with the whole story. On the last but one Shelly had become quite imaginative.

Geez, all Margaret had to do was hide the kid for a few days. She could have given her sleeping tablets. When she woke Margaret would have told about the family's auto accident. "But don't worry," she might have said, "I'm your aunt from America and Mom and Dad said that you could come and live with me." Which five-year-old kid's gonna argue with an adult?

I looked at the most recent email, sent on the Tuesday evening sometime after I'd left. At the top of it was Teresa's original email, still keen for information.

Dear Shel
Do a bit of detective work. Ask the kid about her sister and see what she remembers. Do it when Margaret's not around. We don't want her to know we're on to her.
    Love and kisses Tessa

I rolled my eyes at the endearments and looked at the reply.

Dear Tessa
I did what you asked. I took Judy out to the drugstore for a soda and we had a chat. I said I was doing a study on London and wondered if she had any memories for me. She shook her head. "I was only five," she said, "when my family got killed." I felt awful. Like I might upset the kid. But after a little while she said, "I don't hardly remember a thing from back then. Except for my dog."

I perked up. This American Judy remembered a dog.

She said he was big and slobbery. She loved him to death. She doesn't remember what they called him. She thinks he had longish hair and was brown or maybe brown with white spots. She says he definitely had long ears. Anyway. I'll keep digging.

Love and more kisses Shelly

I read it over again. A big dog. Brown-and-white with long ears. All things that could be attributed to Toby. We never thought of him as particularly big, but then Judy was only a toddler when we got him and only five when she disappeared. For those few years he could have seemed enormous to her.

The tables around me were filling up with students, some whispering while looking over to make sure the library staff didn't see them. I nodded at some people from my classes and noticed that they veered away from me and sat on a distant table. They didn't feel comfortable with me, I knew. I didn't concern myself with teenage issues like sex and boys and drugs and jobs. I simply wasn't interested. That's why I got on with Clare. She made no demands on me. We both just rubbed along together: she submerged her family problems into her art; me, I just dived in and out of the past all day long.

I looked at the emails and the photo again. Should I show them to someone? The police? Or my mum and dad? I had a sudden picture of their faces drinking in the news, one minute incredulous, the next hopeful, then dropping with disdain. For what did it all amount to? A thirteen-year-old girl who looked a bit like a computer-enhanced image. The fact that she was English, that her family had been killed and she had been adopted by an American woman. Now it seemed she had a dog that might have been Toby. On our side of the Atlantic a pink fleece top had been found underneath the paving stones of a garden. At the time the garden was laid an American couple were living there.

The connections were thin, like threads across an ocean. Whoever I told would see that. For them it would be as though I had seen another girl and followed her, only to stand forlornly outside her house hoping against hope that she was my sister. Was that all it was? Another of my mistakes? I thought of Pam and what she would say. I could almost see her head slowly shaking, a knowing expression on her face. *This is just a projection of your own hopes*, she would say. *You are willing your sister back into your life. You have to learn to let go*.

But it wasn't just me. Teresa Russell had seen it. Shelly, the American girl, she had picked it up. *What if they were the same girl!* she had said in her email.

Was it possible? That my sister was living in Seattle? I gathered up the emails and the photographs and held them close to my chest. I must have looked funny because the librarian walked in my direction.

"Are you all right, Kim?"

She knew my name. That was the notoriety of having a missing sister. Everyone knew who I was. I nodded my head, gathered up my stuff and left.

# ELEVEN

As soon as I got home I went straight up to the study and turned the computer on. My mum and dad were out and the house was quiet. That was a relief because I didn't want to have to explain what I was doing. I clicked the icon for email and typed in Shelly's address. Then I began to compose my message to her.

Dear Shelly
Teresa Russell told me about you and gave me your email address. I hope you don't mind me making contact. I've read over your messages to Teresa and I'm interested in what you say. I'm not saying I believe in your theory, just that it interests me. Could you talk to this girl some more? Ask her about the accident that her family had. When and where was it? What about the names of her family or photographs of them? Surely her adopted mother has some of these?

I stopped then. The last sentence was sounding a bit desperate. I changed it.

Perhaps her adopted mother has some photographs? I'm really grateful for all this even though, as I say, I don't really think that your neighbour's daughter…

I wanted to say "is my sister" but I couldn't type the words. Instead I put:

has any connection to me or my family.
   Kim Hockney

I clicked the send button and sat back, surprised to find my shoulders tight with tension. I stood up and walked around the small room, looking at my mum and dad's filing cabinet, their photocopier and their fax machine. On the walls were posters for CHILDLOSS, the support group. There were also calendars of events and some newspaper cuttings about the success of the group. There was nothing about my sister. Cuttings about Judy's disappearance were not the sort of thing you displayed on a wall. In fact there was nothing of Judy in there at all, which was surprising because it used to be her bedroom.

In those days it had deep-pink wallpaper covered in cartoon characters. There were shelves of soft toys and, in the corner, an old doll's house that my mum had had as a child. It had been in my bedroom for a while but when Judy became old enough to understand what it was she had wanted it. It hadn't bothered me – I had moved on to other things. I used to hear her playing with it, talking to herself, moving the little figures from one room to the other. It often kept her happy for half an hour or so, but she loved it best of all if someone else played with her. I usually didn't have the time. I was always too busy, reading books, writing stories, talking to my best friend Teresa on the telephone.

I remembered the months after she had gone. I would come up to her room and lie on the bed among her soft toys. I would pull the duvet up over my face and breathe deeply, sure that I could smell Judy from it. It was a smell like sweets, chewy soft strawberry sweets. After a few seconds the aroma seemed to evaporate and I would be left lying there clutching the fabric.

One day I came home from school and found the room had been stripped. Opening the bedroom door and seeing the bare floorboards, the stripped walls, the windowless curtains had sent me reeling. I had cried for hours. Mum and Dad had explained. They were putting Judy's room to good use. It was going to be the base for the support group – a way of keeping Judy's name in the public eye and helping other families at the same time.

All her *important* things, they said, were in the loft.

So it was an office, a business space, a place where people spent time tapping keys or talking on the telephone. It no longer held the memory of my sister. Like the doll's house that had been put into storage.

A noise from downstairs made me go out into the hall. It was the sound of the front door closing. I thought it was my mum or dad but the sound of my aunt's voice carried up the stairs.

"Anyone home?" she shouted.

"I'm here," I replied.

I went downstairs to see her rubbing her hands

together at the radiator. Her coat was wet. It had started to rain and I hadn't noticed.

"I'm glad I've caught you," she said. "I wanted to have a word. Shall we have a cup of tea?"

Rosie walked ahead of me down the hall. My aunt was a big woman, too heavy for her height, but she moved quickly and always seemed to have bundles of energy. She was five years or so older than my mum but much less confident. While my mum spoke at CHILDLOSS meetings Rosie usually sat mute, her knitting needles clicking furiously, her head nodding at things she agreed with. She was shy in company and it was usually Jeff who spoke and she who agreed with him. She was happiest surrounded by plants and bags of compost, her fingernails thick with soil, her hands and arms grimy. When she wasn't working or in our house she spent time in a charity shop where she sold her handmade knitted jumpers.

She was relaxed with me and Mum and I liked her a lot.

She went straight to the kettle and started to fill it, opening and shutting cupboard doors to get the tea things out. All the time she was asking me about college and my course and my *nice friend* Clare. I sat and watched her moving with ease around our kitchen. Why not? It was like a second home to her.

She and Jeff were childless, but not through choice. Rosie had had a miscarriage a short while after Judy disappeared. Everybody said it was due to stress, but

Rosie insisted it had just been one of those unexplained things. Since then there had never been any talk of pregnancy or babies. Rosie often said it didn't bother her. She said she was too busy helping Jeff to run their plant nursery. She was very close to my mum and even before Judy's disappearance she had always visited regularly, dropping by, usually with plastic trays of pansies or impatiens or bags of compost or hanging baskets. Our garden was always buzzing with colour.

After Judy went missing my aunt and uncle were around a lot. In those days they had a part-time assistant at the nursery, a pensioner called Frank Lewis. He had been left to run the business over the winter months while Rosie and Jeff took root in our house, a constant comfort for my mum and dad. That was when the miscarriage happened. Then, in the following spring, Frank had a heart attack and had to retire, and their business almost collapsed. It was my parents who had their daughter taken away from them, but Rosie and Jeff's life seemed to fall apart as well. My mum gave Rosie and Jeff a key and told them to come round whenever they felt like it. They got involved in CHILDLOSS and seemed to spend as much time round our house as they did in their own. As the years went by it lessened, but they were still regular visitors, my Aunt Rosie more so. My Uncle Jeff went back to building up the business.

"We wondered if you felt like coming to stay with us for a while, maybe in the Christmas holidays? There's masses to do in the nursery and we could pay you a bit so that you could earn some money."

Rosie poured the boiling water into the teapot. She was one of the few people I knew who still did that. My mum and dad and me, we usually just put a tea bag in a cup and covered it in boiling water.

"What do you think?" she said, brightly.

I nodded my head politely. My aunt and uncle's nursery was a comfortable place to be. They had a big old house that had once been the centre of a farm. Over the years the land had been sold off and they'd bought the remains; the farmhouse and the ten acres that surrounded it. Their kitchen was huge, with a stone floor and a giant wooden table. A big window overlooked the nursery car park and the long greenhouses behind which held the stock. There was a tiny shop which doubled up as an office, and whenever any customers arrived my aunt or uncle would take their place behind the till. Sometimes we would be sitting drinking tea at the kitchen table and watch as a car pulled up outside, and then the three of us would rush out to see who could get to the shop first. They didn't do great business but it was fun being there.

"What about Mum and Dad?"

"They could come and pick you up on Christmas Eve. To tell you the truth, you'd be doing me a real favour. Jeff isn't what you'd call good company at the moment. There's some talk about a new supermarket development and there's a rumour that there'll be a garden centre attached. I don't think he's had a complete night's sleep for weeks. Oh, listen to me! What are our little troubles compared to…"

Her voice drained away. That's how it had always been. Whatever troubles anyone else had, they were never as big as ours. I felt sorry for her though. My Uncle Jeff hadn't seemed his old self lately. I nodded my head. Why not spend a bit of time with them? Christmas was a long way off.

"I could teach you to drive," Rosie said, smiling and pushing a mug of tea in my direction. "You said you wanted to learn."

I perked up. I did want to learn how to drive. The nursery was offroad and had tracks around the greenhouses. That meant I could start to learn the basics without having to worry about the rest of the traffic.

"There's the nursery, of course, but there's also this disused airfield a couple of kilometres down the road. We could go there."

"Yes, I'd like that," I said, picturing myself at the wheel of a car.

"Only what with everything happening … about Judy… We thought it might be good for you to have a change of scenery."

Why did she say that? For a few moments I hadn't been thinking about Judy. I had visualized myself in the country, amid the frost – and perhaps even snow – of Christmas. The three of us selling Christmas trees and me getting the "L" plates out, sticking them on to the front of Rosie or Jeff's car. Just the visit of a niece to her uncle and aunt.

But it wasn't that at all. It was a scheme put together to get me out of the way. In case the find in the garden of Willow Drive turned into something more upsetting. I was being tucked away somewhere like a piece of delicate china that might shatter if handled too roughly. No doubt my mum and dad were in on the plan as well. *It might be better to get Kim out of the way...*

From behind I heard the front door opening and the sound of my mum and dad talking. Their voices were low, my dad's a little husky.

"We're in here," Rosie sang out.

They came into the kitchen, long-faced, still wearing their coats, little splashes of rain showing on their shoulders.

"Any news?" Rosie said, getting two more mugs out of the cupboard.

My mum shook her head and sat down on a chair. She looked tired, her cheekbones prominent. She was too thin, I thought. My dad started to unbutton his coat and took a deep breath.

"They're still doing forensic tests on the top. They'll let us know if there's a DNA match."

"I'm sure there will be," my mum said. "I have this feeling. This is Judy's top. It makes sense. She was on that road and..."

I had this sudden image of my sister pausing on Willow Drive. It was dark and she was unsure of where she was going. She could have turned and walked up someone's garden path. That's why they never found a trace of her. The front door of a house could have opened and swallowed her up. The American woman's house. I felt my fingers tapping frantically on the side of my mug. The woman had perhaps been looking out of her window and seen a small child walking along in the dark. She had gone outside and persuaded her to come in. *Why don't you come in and I'll telephone your mummy*, she might have said. Judy might have gone in, talking all the way, moaning about her big sister and her friend who wouldn't play with her.

My mum and dad had sat down at opposite ends of the table. Their faces were heavy with worry. Rosie was still chattering, making herself busy by emptying the teapot and sloshing it round with boiling water.

*What if Judy is really alive and living in America?* I wanted to say. I almost had my mouth open to say it.

"Trouble is," my mum said, "what about the red van? The police believed – they still do believe – that that was an important clue."

"If they could just link it to this house in some way," my dad said. "Then we'd be getting somewhere."

I closed my eyes. I was back in Willow Drive, peering into the empty street. There it was, coming towards me, the red van: glowing in the night, shimmering like a mirage in a desert. How many times had I wished it was real? How often had I tried to persuade myself that I really had seen something? But it wasn't true. I only had to open my eyes and it would dissolve into mist.

I didn't speak. I left them there and went upstairs to the computer. I turned it back on and logged on to the email service. I put my password in and waited. I was tense watching the screen, my finger tapping lightly across the keys. After a few seconds the words came up. No new messages.

It was too soon. I knew that. Feeling foolish, I turned it all off and went into my room.

# TWELVE

I woke up in the middle of the night and couldn't get back to sleep. My duvet felt like it was weighted with lead and, after wrestling with it for what seemed like hours, I got up and found myself getting ready to go up to the loft.

I made sure everything was quiet and that my mum and dad's light was out. The radiators were stone cold so I put my woolly jogging bottoms and socks on under my dressing gown. I knew it would be cold up there. I tiptoed out along the landing and opened the door that led to the loft stairs. I stepped carefully, expecting sudden creaks from the unused boards, my hand lightly touching the plastered walls, steadying myself for the sharp turn in the stairs that led to the loft.

Once inside the long room I stood very still, listening hard in case there was any movement from downstairs. There wasn't a sound. I didn't turn the light on, I just waited until my eyes had got used to the dark. There was a bright moon outside and it threw a blue hue across the middle of the floor. The boards were hard underfoot and the smell of wood and plaster dust was still there, even after eight years. Or perhaps it wasn't. Possibly that was in my head, a sensory memory from the past. For it was a long time since I had been up there, not since I'd started seeing Pam.

It was fuller now. I noticed several new cardboard boxes stacked along the wall next to some fold-up chairs and boxes of books. Most of it was CHILDLOSS stuff. There were also some old dining chairs and a sofa that had seen better days. I walked quietly over to one of the tiny dormer windows that looked out on to the street far below. The wood around the frame had never been painted and still looked new. I turned the tiny brass handle and opened the window. The cold air came bristling in, making me hug myself and blink my eyes a few times. I leaned out and looked into the street below. I could see the tops of the trees that lined the pavement. Dotted among them were the streetlights that looked like yellow lollipops. Below, through the foliage, I could see the roofs of cars. There was even a van – not red, just a light colour, parked carelessly at an angle.

Over the years I did try to tell people about the van. At first, when the police hadn't been able to find it, I felt a surge of relief. Even though I was only nine, almost ten, I knew that I'd told a terrible lie. The search had been relentless and a lot of people had been interviewed, one man even kept in a cell overnight. I thought then that the police would give up on the search. *Perhaps it might not have been red?* I'd said tentatively. *Or maybe I'd not seen it on that night? I'd confused it with another night, a different van, or possibly it was a car. A red car, not a van at all, and those registration numbers were not an X and a P but an E and a B?*

*No, no*, the police insisted. *I had to trust the memory I had on the night of the reconstruction. I was only unsure because they hadn't found it. And anyway, they insisted, there was an important point that backed up my sighting of the van and its involvement in the disappearance of my sister. The very fact that the driver hadn't come forward. This showed that he had some guilty secret. He knew that the police were looking for him and his van. If he was innocent, why didn't he just drive up to his local police station?*

*No*, they said, *the red van is the most important clue*.

I could have confessed. I could have told the truth at any time. But as the weeks and months went by the story began to take on a sort of truth of its own. Maybe there had been a red van. Why would I have plucked something like that out of thin air? Very possibly I had seen one and tucked the fact away in my subconscious. I convinced myself over the first year that I had told the truth. It suited everyone.

But on the first anniversary, on the day when I tried to take the child from Sparrow Gardens, when my dad and the police had to prise my fingers from the small girl's arm, I knew then it was all a pack of lies. That's why I became ill. That's why I missed so much school. Everyone else thought it was some kind of post-traumatic stress but it wasn't. I had this awful truth, like some kind of poisonous snake, wriggling around inside me. That's why I agreed to go to counselling sessions with Pam. I thought that, over time, she could charm it out of me, release it, and in doing that make me free again.

But I could never tell her, just like I'd never been able to tell anyone. Those childish words, spoken to please, were carved into me.

I turned away from the window and looked back at the far corner. Judy's corner, where her things had been stacked: her clothes, toys, bedcovers, her doll's house. I fancied I saw myself there, sitting cross-legged on the floor, a girl of ten, eleven, twelve, maybe even fourteen. In those days I visited the loft during the daytime, the grey light spilling in through the tiny windows; my head bent, my arms full of some of my sister's things: her dresses, her soft toys, her books. On many occasions I simply sat and played with her doll's house, tidying up the furniture and moving it into different rooms. The front of the house opened like a door and I would reach in, my huge fingers picking up the tiny figures and making them walk across a room or sit in a chair or lie on a bed. Sometimes I worked with the figures on the ground floor, sitting them all down around the television. Closing the front I would look through each window, like some curious giant.

The loft had been finished a couple of months before Judy disappeared. Part of it was meant to be a study for my dad, where he could do his accounts for the bread shop. The rest was to be a play area for me and Judy. My mum had plans for desks and computers, paints and dressing-up boxes. She was going to buy a sewing machine, she said, and teach us how to make our own clothes. There was plenty of room, she said; after they had built a dividing wall for Dad's study the rest was ours. But it never happened. The loft conversion itself was finished, all that was needed was the dividing wall and the decorating. That should have started the week that Judy went missing.

My mum and dad left it. A long empty room, with odd sloping shoulders, pink plaster walls the colour of skin, the floorboards untrodden and curtainless windows that looked naked from inside.

I walked across to Judy's things and found that they'd been tidied up by someone, packed into neat boxes with labels on the outside: clothes, books, toys. The doll's house still stood proudly, its pieces gathering dust inside. I squatted down and had to pull it gently by the sides because it had been turned around, the front facing the wall. I took care not to make any noise, and when it was done I stood up and pulled off one of the sofa cushions and laid it on the floor to sit on.

It was too dark to see what was going on inside but I opened the door anyway, and looked in each room, making out some of the toy pieces and the figures.

Then I sat back and wondered why I had come. One of my first resolutions with Pam had been to leave this stuff alone. *How many times do you go up to the loft?* she'd said. *It depends*, I'd answered, *three or four times a week*. But I'd been lying. Sometimes, if I was feeling fretful, I would go up there every day. I'd kept it hidden from Mum and Dad. It was like a kind of addiction where I had to sort through and tidy up Judy's things.

I had got over that stage, hadn't I?

I pulled my dressing gown tightly around me and noticed my breath in little clouds in the air. I looked round and saw the window still open. I got up and closed it my arms shivering now with the cold. I was wide awake. I sat on the old sofa and saw that the doll's house from that angle looked suddenly different. It was standing just outside the beam of moonlight and looked mysterious and outlandish.

I thought for a moment that it looked like an American house. The type that's built from white clapboard, detached, standing alone amid a lawn and trees. I thought then of my sister living in a house like that, in Seattle, next-door to Shelly and her family. I imagined this thirteen-year-old girl talking about *garbage* instead of rubbish and using *elevators* instead of lifts. She'd have braces on her teeth and drink coffee instead of tea.

I found myself smiling at these things and glanced at the old doll's house again. I imagined her running out of her front door towards the yellow school bus that collected her and took her to some Junior High School. She'd talk about her sophomore year and she'd support the baseball team. Knowing Judy, knowing how she'd liked the limelight, she'd be some kind of cheerleader, dancing and singing in scanty clothes. I imagined that Margaret, her adopted mother, would look out of the window of the clapboard house, waiting impatiently for Judy to come home, nervously rubbing her hands together, some cookies and milk waiting on the side.

I pulled my knees up and laid my head on the arm of the chair. I was feeling pleasantly sleepy. The beam of light from the window seemed paler, with just a hint of the morning. My sister in America. Why not? I saw her among a group of girls of her own age and it gave me a warm feeling. My body felt heavy, drowsy. Perhaps she would be studious, working away at her classes, wearing her own clothes to school, having a locker in a corridor and carrying her math books. I could see her smiling and laughing. I could almost hear her speaking.

Was it then that I started to really believe that my sister was living in America? The girl at the barbecue, holding the neck chain with the letter "J"; the computer image of Judy as she would look now. They did match; it was only my reluctance that stopped me from seeing it.

Then there was Toby, the dog.

I so much wanted it to be true. Who wouldn't?

# THIRTEEN

I didn't get an immediate reply. I logged on on Saturday morning and afternoon and just before I went to bed. Each time the phrase No new messages flashed up at me. I felt myself becoming irritable with the machinery, banging the keys down and pushing the off button with more force than necessary. While the systems were connecting I was breathing shallowly, waiting tensely to see if I had a message.

Eventually, on Sunday morning, the words One new message came up. I felt a flutter of excitement and leaned forward to read the words carefully.

Dear Kim,

Tessa told me how nice you were and how you and she used to hang out together. I'm not surprised that you're interested in my neighbor Margaret. Ever since she moved in next-door to us I always thought she was odd. A bit secretive. Like the clothes she wears. They're really old-fashioned. They cover her up from head to toe even in the summer. And she wears like really heavy panstick make-up, like she's trying to disguise something. Geez, I don't mind doing a bit of detective work. She doesn't mind poking her nose into my life. Just because she works in a pharmacy she thinks she knows everything there is to know about drugs and she's always telling my mom about the perils of young people and alcohol, pills and stuff. It really gets on my nerves. I'll get back to you when I've got some news.

   Yours helpfully,
   Shelly

I could just imagine what Shelly was like. I remembered her waving to the camera in the photograph that Teresa passed on to me. She looked bouncy, as if she hardly ever stood still. I imagined that she was popular at school, little groups of girls appearing around her whenever she set foot in the door. For some reason this irked me, but I put my feelings to one side. I wasn't looking for a lifelong friendship.

In the last few days the atmosphere inside my house had changed. When the pink top had been discovered there was optimism – any information was better than eight years of silence. But since then there had been a lot of toing and froing and phone calls from the police. The forensic tests on the top were continuing and there was palpable tension; my mum and dad were steeling themselves for bad news.

I myself spent a lot of my time thinking about the American girl. The story was growing inside my head, developing a life of its own. I was feeling lighter somehow, fresher, and I had more energy than I'd had for weeks. As my mum and dad's movements seemed heavier and more laboured, I had a virtual skip in my step.

During Sunday lunch my dad got another call from

the police. We'd been eating a chicken casserole, one of those ready-made ones with small onions and red wine. There were jacket potatoes that had been in the oven too long, their skins like tough paper which crackled when we cut into them. None of us were eating much, and when the phone rang my dad sprang up and disappeared for a few moments. My mum and I continued eating but we were both listening hard to my dad's answers out in the hallway. By the time he got back to the table my mum had laid her knife and fork together and sat back.

"That was Inspector Robbins. They've managed to get hold of the people who owned the house in Willow Drive eight years ago. The old lady is long dead, of course, but it was her son who organized the letting of the house. He's been very helpful, the police said."

"And?" my mum questioned.

She wasn't looking good. She still had her smart clothes on, make-up on her face and her hair washed and blown dry. But something indefinable was wrong. Her skin looked dry, one of her earrings was twisted, her mascara had smudged under one eye. There was a heavy aroma of perfume, sickly sweet as though she'd sprayed too much on – a sort of camouflage.

"Her son remembers the tenants. There were two, but he thought they weren't a couple, they were just sharing the house. The man was English and the woman was American. They were both at the same college, apparently, some sort of science students, he thought. It was only for six months and the man moved out a month or so before the end of the tenancy. The woman stayed on until the end. She was going travelling, he said, to Europe and then back to the States."

I chewed my chicken slowly, not tasting any of it.

"Does he have a name, an address, anything like that?" my mum said with impatience.

"Yes, the name on the tenancy agreement was Ann Carter, and he thought she came from one of the southern states, Florida or Alabama. But that's all. They've faxed all the stuff through to the American police. Now they're looking into the origins of the paving stones. If they can find who provided the materials for the garden work that might help."

My dad was looking better. As though the information had given him a boost. My mum seemed to sink lower in her chair, using one finger to push her plate further away from her. The ringing of the phone broke the quiet and she got up to go and answer it. Within a few seconds she was in a conversation with someone. Taking a mouthful of powdery potato, I thought about what my dad had said. The woman and man were not a couple, they were students sharing a house. The man left first and the woman went travelling. This was what Shelly's neighbour did. As well as that she worked in a pharmacy, perhaps dispensing drugs. The woman in Willow Drive had been studying science.

So many coincidences. It was hard to dismiss them all.

Shelly sent a second email late that night. I opened it up to check before I got ready for bed. It was longer and more detailed.

Dear Kim,

Lots to tell you. I took Judy out to the mall this afternoon. Her mom, Margaret, gave her some money to buy a jacket. She was really grateful that I was going along. Geez, she was quite nice to me which is unusual. Anyhow me and Judy walked around all the stores and she must've tried a dozen jackets on. While we did it I was casually asking her about her past. She doesn't remember much before she lived with Margaret (apart from the dog). She says her parents and sister, who was called Kate, were killed when their car crashed with a lorry in Oxford Street on Christmas Eve (which is sad if that's what really happened). She says she has photos and I asked, in a casual way, whether I could have a look at one of them.

I stopped reading then. I glanced back and looked at the sister's name. Kate. It wasn't a million miles from my own name, Kim.

I read on.

She says she's never seen their graves or been back to England. She says that Margaret is going to take her on a tour of Europe after she graduates. I asked her what Margaret is like. She says Margaret is great, lots of fun, but overprotective. She won't let her go to summer camp or on any sleepovers. She says it's probably because of the way Suzie, her other child, died in the swimming-pool accident. I asked her when it was she died but she wasn't sure. I had to be careful because she looked at me a bit funny and said, "What's with you and the third degree?" So I stopped then and we got her jacket (quilted with a zipper – gorgeous). I'll let you know if I hear any more or if she shows me the photograph.

Love Shelly

I printed off the emails and then deleted them from my message board. Then I turned the computer off. I heard the front door slamming as I went into my own room. My mum and dad were back from yet another visit to the police station. It sounded as though my Aunt Rosie was with them as well. I went downstairs.

My mum looked wretched, her eyes with great dark shadows under them. My Aunt Rosie was sitting beside her. I looked at my dad for an explanation.

"The pink top is definitely Judy's. The police matched some DNA samples ... some saliva and stuff..."

So it was my sister's top. I didn't speak. I watched my mum crying and realized that I, too, should have been upset. Strangely though, I wasn't. They thought that the finding of the top meant that Judy was dead. But for me it was the opposite. It meant that Judy had gone into that house where the American woman had stayed. Could this American woman be Margaret? And Judy, the girl who was, at that very moment, wearing her new quilted zip-up jacket, could she be our Judy, all grown-up? *Why not?* I thought, smug with myself, my confidence blooming.

They were all looking at me strangely, my mum's eyes screwed up as if she couldn't believe what she was seeing. And then I realized. They'd just told me the most important news about Judy in eight years and I had a wide smile on my face.

How could they help but be upset? If only they had known.

# FOURTEEN

I was sitting in front of the computer at six-thirty the next morning. It was still dark outside, although I could hear the sounds of traffic in the distance and from nearby the noise of the radiators juddering and clanking as the central heating came on. I didn't notice the cold as I tapped my password into the keyboard. The usual phrase, No new messages, came up and I huffed. I told myself that Seattle was halfway round the world, even though I knew that distance made no difference with emails. It made a difference in other ways, though. I felt suddenly aware of this great landmass between us, thick and impenetrable. Plus there was the ocean, a giant wall of water that moved and shifted, yet stood still enough to hold the countries apart. That was why it was so perfect. Take a girl off the street in one place and transport her to somewhere else. Everyone was looking for a man: a man who loved little girls so much he wanted to kill them. No one was looking for a woman who was replacing one child with another.

I was becoming impatient, I knew that. I was hungry for more information and it wasn't there yet. I had no choice but to wait. I disconnected and went out to the landing. I could hear my dad snoring lightly and the sound of my mum moving around. I didn't particularly want her to see me up so early, so I slipped back into my bedroom and lay on top of the covers.

I thought about the day ahead. The police investigation into the house in Willow Drive was stepping up. Every centimetre of the garden would be dug up and the inside of the house – the floorboards, the cellar, the loft – all these places would be searched for any further clues. My mum and dad were going to be on hand all day; *for as long as it takes*, my dad had said, through clenched teeth. I had offered to stay at home but he'd looked distantly at me and told me to go on to college.

I had ample time for breakfast and a shower before going to college. In the end I had neither. I waited till Mum and Dad were in the kitchen and then I went back on to the computer and sat there staring at the screen, willing a message to come through. After a while I went downstairs and got a mug of tea, and when I came back there it was. One new message. I felt thrilled. It was long and detailed, and I only glanced over it. I kept looking round in case anyone came into the room, so I printed it off to take to college with me.

I walked all the way, enjoying the cold air on my face. When I got to college I was momentarily disorientated. I had a number of lessons timetabled but I had no intention of going to them. I made my way to the library and found an empty desk. The study area was unusually full of students and I found myself in the middle of a group of lads who were pretending to look at giant maths books and playing with text messages on their mobiles under the desks, breaking into silent giggles from time to time. I found it easy to ignore them. I opened my bag and pulled out the email and it was as if I was in a sealed cube; their physical closeness, their noise didn't touch me as I read Shelly's message.

Dear Kim,

I'm doing this in the middle of the night. My folks have gone to bed. I'm in big trouble with them and it's all Margaret's fault. After supper I went round there to see what Judy was doing. She asked me up to her bedroom. That's the nice thing about Judy. She seems to have a bit of a crush on me. I think she likes hanging around with older kids. (Margaret was in the basement, I think she has a study down there.) So, we're in Judy's room, and I continue gently asking her about her life in England. She's more interested in trying the new jacket on and pulls a ton of clothes out of her closet to try on. I'm sitting there and saying which one goes with the jacket and which doesn't. All the time I'm like, "So which part of London did you live in with your folks?" And, "So where did you first live when you came to the States?"

I found out a few new things.

1. She said she lived north of the River Thames. (I always want to pronounce this wrong, with a "th" sound!)

2. When she first came to the States she and Margaret lived somewhere really hot and there were crocodiles. (I take it from this that she lived in Florida. And they're not crocodiles, they're alligators.)

3. She remembers some things about her real parents. She

said her mom was cuddly and had beautiful hair. Her dad was the tallest dad in her school and he...

I stopped reading for a moment. I thought of a five-year-old child craning her neck to look up at her dad. I thought of my mum's hair, years ago, when Judy had been a toddler. It had been long and curly with untidy strands flying out. Nowadays, as well as being thinner, my mum had had her hair cut into a neat bob.

My concentration was thrown for a moment by a couple of the boys around me, sniggering loudly at something. The librarian was over the other side of the room but she was looking in our general direction to see where the bubble of noise was coming from. I went back to the email.

Her dad was the tallest dad in her school and he always smelled of sweet things. After she told me these things she said, "We have photos, do you want to see?" So naturally I said, "Yes, of course," and I followed her along to her mother's room. Honestly, Kim, this was the tidiest bedroom I have ever seen. There wasn't a single thing out of place, not even a housecoat hanging on the back of the bedroom door. Geez, you should see my mom and dad's bedroom. Anyway, she stands up on this stool and gets a box from the top shelf of the closet. She puts it on the bed and takes off the lid. Inside there's these packets of photos, really old, like about ten years or so. Judy has picked out this plastic envelope and she's taking these pictures out. I opened one of the old packets and found these pictures of a small girl, a toddler, looking sweet and happy, and I'm looking at these when she holds up this photo of a man and woman, and two daughters, one about six and the other just a toddler. It's old, taken a while ago. The man and woman are sitting by a tree and the daughters are beside them. There's some sort of picnic and they're not all looking at the camera. I thought, for a minute, that I could sneak it out and email it to you but then, when I turned it over, it had this imprint on the back of the place where it had been developed. And here's the thing, the address was in Florida! It wasn't even an English photograph! Judy was chattering away and pointing the people out. She was the toddler, she said, although I couldn't see much of a resemblance. I didn't say anything, I just found myself flicking through this other packet of photographs, the ones of the little girl. "That's Suzie," Judy says, "Margaret's little girl who was drowned." I felt funny then, kind of nosey, and I was just about to pack them away when I heard Margaret's voice. "What the hell do you think you're doing?" she says and when I turned round she was standing there with her hands on her hips, practically smoking with rage. She ordered me out and told me never to come back! I had to walk out of that room like some kid being sent to the principal's office. And that's not the worst. An hour or so later she came over to talk with my parents. She was in with them a long time and I could hear her voice, loud and angry. When she went I thought the screen door was going to come off its hinges. My mom came up to my room. It seems Margaret wasn't just angry about me being in her bedroom and looking through her photos – it turns out that she'd been getting increasingly worried about Judy lately. The kid had started asking questions about her English parents and getting upset, particularly at night. Margaret hadn't known why, but now Judy's told her that I'd been asking questions because of some English project I'd been doing. Course my mom is mystified, doesn't know anything about an English project, so Margaret blows up and says that I'm just being nosey and should mind my own business, that poor Judy has had a traumatic life and I have no business raking it all up. So Margaret says I am not allowed to talk to Judy any more which Mom thinks is a complete overreaction. I don't, though. I think Margaret knows I'm on to her, that's why she's so upset. What do you think?

Love Shelly

I put the email down on the table and noticed that I was alone. The lads who had been around me were no longer there. They were walking out of the library exit in a little huddle, the librarian walking behind them like an irate policeman. I folded up the email, not sure what I was feeling. The story was growing in my mind. It was like reading bits of a novel over days and weeks – the ending first, sections of the middle, the beginning last – little chunks of a big story that merged together.

I found myself walking out of the library. To tell the absolute truth, I was agitated. I went up to the first floor and looked in the art rooms for Clare. I found her sitting at one of the long windows alongside two other students. They were all sketching. I stood for a minute, not speaking, until she noticed me.

"Hi."

Clare gave me a half smile. She seemed to be looking

hard at me: at my hair, my clothes. The other girls stared as well, and I saw one of them give the other a quizzical look.

I put my hand up and touched my hair. It felt odd, standing up a little. Glancing down at my shirt I saw that it was wrinkled and grubby and the buttons were done up wrongly. I tutted to myself.

"How about some tea?" Clare said, laying down her sketch pad. "We've got a kettle in the office."

I followed her and sat on a stool.

"I was in a rush this morning," I said, realigning the buttons on my shirt and combing my fingers through my hair.

"Tell me about it," Clare said. "I'm terrible in the morning."

"How are things?" I said, remembering her difficult home situation.

"Not too bad. Freddie and my mum are going to buy a new house between them. That means that my dad will have his half of the sale money and he should be able to find a place. I don't suppose they'll ever be friends, you know..."

But I wasn't listening. Her voice just seemed to drift away from me, and I looked down at the email in my hand. I was aware that I was nodding in agreement but the strange thing was I couldn't seem to stop and my head was bouncing gently back and forth. Clare was sitting open-mouthed, looking strangely at me.

"What's wrong, Kim?" she said. "Is it about Judy?"

Straight to the point as usual. I kept nodding and tried to speak, but the words just piled up in my throat. I was looking stupid, I knew. I needed to tell someone, to say the words out loud. *My sister is alive and living in America.* Then it would become more real. The facts would be out there and not just inside my head, not just living in the space between two computers, or in the head of an American girl.

"Is it because they found your sister's top? Are you afraid they'll find her body?"

Clare said it softly, her hand reaching out and covering mine. She had it all wrong. She thought I was worried about finding my sister *dead.* I noticed then the splashes of paint on her fingers, pale, watery colours, blues and greens.

"No, no, quite the opposite," I stammered.

I took a mouthful of scalding hot tea and swallowed it without tasting. I felt it burning all the way down my throat.

"No, you see –" then I lowered my voice to whisper – "I think, I'm almost sure that she's still alive!"

Clare looked crestfallen. I was surprised. I had thought she might be sceptical, who wouldn't? Maybe even incredulous. Instead she looked disappointed in me, as though I had done something wrong. I felt uncomfortable watching her. I wanted to go. I took another drink of the tea then stood up.

"I have to go. Mum and Dad need me…"

She nodded. "I'll give you a lift."

"No, I need the fresh air," I said.

I left her there and walked down the stairs. I almost walked into Teresa Russell and her friends sauntering along the corridor. I ducked back into a classroom, holding my breath until I was sure they were gone. One of my teachers passed by. She looked at me standing clutching the email and I gave her a half smile and walked on.

Once out of the college I felt this sense of relief, as if I was escaping from something. I walked briskly along the road, looking straight ahead. As I got nearer home I quickened my steps until I was almost running. I had this feeling that there would be something there for me, something important. When I got in the house I called out, but no one answered. The breakfast dishes were still on the kitchen table and my mum's bed was empty but unmade. I went straight into the study and logged on to the email.

There it was. One new message. The most important that I'd had from Shelly. I held my breath while I was reading it.

Dear Kim,
You won't believe it. Margaret and Judy are moving house. I overheard my mom talking about it just a while ago. It seems Margaret has decided to move on. She had the realtors around today. Here's the strange thing. It takes a while to sell a house and buy a new one but Margaret is moving the day after tomorrow. She and Judy are doing some sightseeing, apparently, before moving east! I think she's running away.

Trouble is, once she's gone will anyone be able to find her?
  Love Shelly

I stared in shock at the screen. Margaret was going to take Judy away from me for the second time.

# FIFTEEN

I hadn't heard the sound of the front door opening and closing so when I ran downstairs and saw my mum and dad in the living room I was momentarily startled.

"Hello, love," my dad said.

I had the emails in my hand, all of them, and the photos and things that Teresa Russell had passed on to me. I had intended to spread them all out on the living-room table and explain them to my parents when they came back. I must have looked as though I was doing something I shouldn't because they were staring suspiciously at me. I looked a bit of a fright, I knew. I should have changed my clothes, washed my hair, tidied up a bit, but I hadn't had the time. I patted down my blouse and pointed to the wad of stuff I had in my hand.

"I've got something important to show you," I said.

I rushed over to the table and started to lay my things down as though I was dealing a game of cards. I was nervous but it had to be done. Margaret was moving house and was very probably packing up Judy's things at that moment. In a day or two they would slide into a car and zoom off down one of the freeways to some unknown destination.

From behind me I heard the sound of the doorbell. I wasn't worried. It was probably Rosie and Jeff and they were family; anything I had to say could be said in front of them. I stood back and looked at the table. It was all there, all the necessary information. After Mum and Dad had looked at it it would have to be collected up and put in a folder for the police to examine. I saw, in my head, a neat folder with a white label on it. *Judy Hockney*. I could hear hushed voices from the hall, my mum and dad talking to someone else. I turned round to look and there, coming into the living room, was Pam, my counsellor.

I was surprised. I had never seen Pam in my own home before. I had never seen her with my parents, certainly not in conversation with them. I knew that from time to time that she gave them an update, she told me that. But it was always just a couple of words or phrases, like a school report, she'd said: *Kim is making satisfactory progress*. The content of our meetings was always confidential. I knew that. I trusted her.

So I was thrown completely when she walked into my living room. Even more so because she was in her out-of-office clothes: tight jeans and a huge mohair-type stripy jumper. Underneath her jeans I noticed that she had cowboy-style boots. Her hair was loose and there was a tiny braided plait down one side. She looked like she was on her way to a line-dancing class.

My mum and dad looked dull and pale beside her and I felt this growing irritation with them.

"What?" I said, half leaning on the table, keeping my eye on the bits of paper and photographs that I had there.

"Should we go?" my dad said, addressing his words to Pam.

"Perhaps Kim and I could have a quick chat," Pam said, looking quickly at me.

"No," I said, pointing at the table, "I've got some things to show you."

None of them spoke. The three of them looked uneasy. Especially my mum. She was wearing this new tracksuit. It wasn't the sort you bought to play sports or keep fit. It was for casual wear and had a matching stripe down the arm and leg. She'd combed her hair back and had no make-up on. I tried to catch her eye, to give her a smile, but she looked away. And then I got it. I understood. They'd brought Pam round here to talk to me, to counsel me. For a moment I felt utterly deflated. They thought I was still sick. How would I ever persuade them that my sister was alive and living in America?

"I'll make some tea," my dad said, but I put my arm out to stop him.

"No," I hissed, "you have to look at this stuff. I've found something out."

"Kim, love." My dad stood beside me and put his arm around my shoulder, "We've found something out as well. That's why we brought Pam around. So that we could all talk about it."

"No, no," I said, shaking him off, "This is important," I said. "I've found out something—"

"Why don't we all sit down? Around the table?" Pam

said, her voice as smooth as butter.

We all did what we were told. Pam smiled encouragingly at us and we moved to the table, the chairs scraping along the floor as my parents pulled them out. My dad sat up straight and my mum leaned her chin on her hands. Pam spoke.

"You tell us what you've got to say, Kim. We won't interrupt."

She was sitting with her hands loosely clasped. I glimpsed her earrings then, small birds that swung back and forth at her chin, sometimes nesting in her hair, sometimes flying out. I couldn't take my eyes off them, and then I noticed the silence. They were waiting for me to speak. I fidgeted with the papers and cleared my throat. My mum and dad were scanning the things I had on the table. In the middle was the photograph of the barbecue, the only proper picture I had of Judy. My mum reached out and pulled it towards her.

"I think I've found Judy," I said, blankly.

There was no point in unfolding it slowly like some treasure map. I had this story and they needed to know what was at the heart of it. I looked at each of them. The only one who showed any feeling was Pam; a look of concern fluttered across her face and then was gone.

"She's alive. I'm sure she is. And she's living in America."

My mum turned away. Her skin was the colour of vanilla ice cream, her expression cold.

"Mum, she's alive. That American woman who lived

in Willow Drive, she took her back to Florida. She snatched her off the street and kept her for a few days. I don't know, maybe she used sleeping tablets... I'm not sure, but she hid her, and when the coast was clear she took her on a plane to America. She had another passport. She told her we were dead, you see. Judy thinks her English family was killed in a road accident. She thinks the American woman is a relative who has adopted her. Look, here, the photo of the American girl and the computer image. Don't they look alike? Don't they?"

I found myself leaning across the table top, my voice squeaky. My mum's lips were quivering but the rest of her face was blank. My dad and Pam were looking searchingly at me. The table was cluttered, my emails and bits of paper askew. I wanted nothing more at that moment than to straighten them, to tidy it all up.

"I didn't think this up," I said, more calmly. "You ask Teresa Russell. She was the one who first suggested it. I didn't believe it. Not at all. But since then, since the find in Willow Drive..."

My dad stood up and put his hand on my shoulder.

"I want you to sit back and listen, Kim. We've got something very important to tell you. Something that might change your mind about all this."

He gestured with his hand at my stuff. He didn't just mean my bits of paper. He meant my story as well. He'd hardly given it a chance and he was dismissing it. I looked at my mum's profile. She'd physically turned herself away. She was having nothing to do with it either. The two of them hadn't even given it a chance. They hadn't read the emails or looked properly at the pictures. They'd hardly let me get the words out of my mouth before they'd buried them quietly with their disdain. Disappointment weighed me down and I sat back in my chair. I looked at Pam who had started to tidy up the papers, her bird earrings diving back and forth, her silly striped sweater jarring in front of me. My dad's voice was scratchy when he spoke.

"Kim, the police have found evidence … they think it's almost certain that Judy is dead."

"No," I shook my head, my face breaking into a smile.

It was the pink top he was talking about. He thought it meant that Judy was dead, but I knew that this was a further link with the American woman. I was shaking my head, my face beaming with confidence.

"They've found forensic evidence—"

"No, no. Look, I know that the top is hers. I know that, but it doesn't mean that she's dead. It's just a top. When Judy went into the house the American woman made her take it off."

"And her skirt and a shoe," my mum snorted.

That shook me but I didn't stop.

"Along with the rest of her things. Of course she did… She bought new clothes for Judy, before she took her to America."

My dad's hand was on my arm. It wasn't an

affectionate gesture. He was holding it still, shushing me all the time I was talking. My mum was sitting rigid, her expression different, her face like a deep pool, flat and dark.

"Judy is dead," my dad said, softly. "We've got to face it."

"No, no," I shook myself free. "NO, SHE'S NOT!"

My mum turned suddenly. Using her arm she swept the table clear, slicing through the photos and emails. Her face was turned towards me.

"Will you stop this!" my mum said. "WILL YOU STOP THIS!"

"You don't understand," I whispered, shaken by her anger. "She's alive. She's living in America with this woman, Margaret. But they're going to move. We'll lose her if we don't."

"Haven't I got enough to worry about?" she shouted. "Isn't losing my daughter enough? Do you have to make it worse every time?"

"What?" I felt this horrible jelly feeling inside.

"Every time we start to pull ourselves together; every little development. Aren't these things enough for us to worry about? On top of it all we need to make sure you don't go completely crackers as well."

"Now, now…" Pam said.

"It's true!" my mum insisted. "We can't cope with this. Time after time. When will you accept it, Kim? Judy's dead."

"But the clothes by themselves. That proves nothing!" I said.

"But what about the blood that was on them? WHAT ABOUT THE BLOOD?" my mum screamed.

I sat very still. Something was clutching at my stomach, twisting it hard, and I could almost hear the pulse pounding in my temple, in my neck, at my wrist. Yet the room itself was calm and quiet, the pages and the photos lying gently on the floor. The faces were hushed and pale, even my mum had become a kind of still life, looking at me and waiting for me to react.

"They've made a forensic match. The blood was Judy's. Something happened to her. Very possibly in that house," my dad said.

Blood on her skirt. I felt weak as paper.

"Maybe there was just a struggle…" I said. There was no conviction in my voice, my words faint and unreadable.

"The police are looking for the man who was staying there. After moving out of the house he came back to work on the garden. And here's the most exciting thing," my dad said, as though he was talking about a bit in a film that he had seen, "when he turned up he was driving a red van. Some of the neighbours remember it."

The red van.

I stood up and tried to turn away from the table. I stumbled a little and had to hold on to the back of the chair to steady myself.

"She's upset," Pam said. "It's only to be expected."

My dad answered her, but I didn't hear his words. I closed my eyes and covered my face with my hands. It was too much, too much to carry round with me. I felt my mum's hands on my arms and smelled the faint scent of her perfume.

"It'll be all right," she whispered. "It'll be hard. There's no doubt. The next few weeks will be the worst. But it's all coming together. The man in the house. He worked on the garden and he was driving a red van."

"No," I said, shaking my head. "No, it's not right."

I couldn't let it go on. For eight years I'd told this lie and it had lain heavily on me; a great lead weight that hung like a pendant round my neck, making me tired and weak and hopeless.

"There was no red van," I said, looking at my mum.

"No, there was. Some of the neighbours remember it. It was parked outside when he was doing the garden. The police think they may even have checked it over."

"No van." I shook my head.

"Kim, there was, love. This is it. This could be the big link."

"You don't understand," I stood back from my mum, pushing her hands away from me. "There never was a red van. I made it up!"

The three of them stood looking at me, their faces quizzical, then one by one, their expressions dropped.

"I made it up. I never saw a red van. I wanted to help. I wanted to find Judy. I tried to remember everything I saw but none of it helped. All I wanted to do was to help find Judy. But I didn't see anything. Nothing. She just disappeared. One minute she was there and the next she was gone, like she'd fallen down some endless hole in the ground." My voice was speeding up, like an express train. "I don't know what happened to her. I didn't see anything suspicious, not a soul. I didn't hear anything. I just lost her. I just lost her. I know it was me who lost her!"

"But the red van?" my mum said, a tiny sparkle of hope in her eyes.

"I made it up. It wasn't true. There was no red van."

She seemed to wither in front of me, her legs buckling as she stepped back to hold on to the table. My dad put his arm around her and they stood together, a pair of sentries, their pain aimed in my direction. Only Pam was unsure and she flapped about for a moment before swooping towards me.

I turned and went out of the room. I heard my mum's voice like lead bullets behind me.

"Let her go."

I opened the front door and went out.

# SIXTEEN

I walked around for most of the afternoon. I went to the local library and glanced over what was left of the day's papers. I sat in the bus garage and watched while the queues slowly built up and then disappeared into a bus, its big engines wheezing with the effort of carrying so many. I walked up and down the old high street where most of the shops had closed and moved to the new indoor centre down the road. I wandered in and out of the charity shops, gazing at rows of dusty secondhand clothes and piles of read books.

Part of me was attentive, looking and taking notice of things. Inside, though, there was a column of ice, cold and hard; all my feelings, my excitement, anticipation, my guilt and my sorrow, all of them frozen.

I found a pound coin in my jacket pocket and bought tea in a polystyrene cup from a baker's and walked along drinking it, feeling the steam warm my nose and cheeks. The weather was cold but fresh. Above me a pale-blue sky was racing past. In the distance I saw some streaks of red on the horizon and I knew it would be getting dark soon.

I'd picked up my coat on my way out but left my bag, purse, mobile phone, everything else upstairs on my bed. All I had was a couple of tissues and the change from a pound coin. I pushed my hands further into my pockets to keep them warm. I'd walked for kilometres, it seemed and I felt better. But I couldn't go home. I couldn't look at any of them now that they knew the truth.

I walked in the direction of Sparrow Gardens, the small park where I'd taken Judy from time to time. The light was fading and the play area was deserted except for two small boys on bikes. I walked to the far end, away from the road, and sat on a bench that bordered an area of trees and bushes. I could see everything from where I was sitting, the swings, the climbing frame and the seesaw. Although it wasn't particularly windy the swings were not still; to me they seemed to be moving, gently undulating against the grey afternoon, the boys on bikes lazily riding by, their backs straight, no hands on the handlebars.

It was a park that I had used as a small child, and when the boys had gone and it was completely empty I imagined noises from all those years ago, like a soundtrack in my head. Many children's voices talking, shouting, squealing even. A distant cry of dismay from someone who had fallen over. A mother calling for a child to be careful on the swings. A dog barking, and in the distance an ice cream van.

Now the park was empty and silent and still the swings seemed to float backwards and forwards. Behind them, on the road, a police car glided by. I felt my neck tighten. I remembered the time a couple of weeks before, when I'd followed the small girl and stood in her street and the police had picked me up. I didn't want that to happen again. I got up from the bench, and in the deepening gloom of the late afternoon I walked back into the bushes and found a place to sit at the foot of a tree. I could still see through the foliage out on to the playground, and even on to the road beyond. I hugged my knees and covered my mouth with my hand, feeling my hot breath against my skin.

I felt comfortable like that. My legs and feet had been cold but I stopped noticing it. My eyes slowly got used to the darkness and I could still make out the shapes of cars and people walking by across the other side of the park. When the street lights suddenly came on I was startled. It gave me something to look at, though. A yellow glow in the distance, and as the evening progressed the lights from different houses popped on and looked like pinprick dots against the dark shadows. Looking up, I could see the moon like a silver coin in the sky, the stars scattered carelessly about like glitter dust.

I even felt happy there for a while. The trees and bushes were tightly round me, like some sort of blanket, and it was ages before the iciness in the air started to sear away at my skin. It didn't matter, though. There, in that park, I couldn't do anything wrong or stupid. I couldn't upset anyone. Most of all, I couldn't lose anything, like I'd lost my sister.

I didn't cry. Most people in that position might have, but I couldn't. It was the bitter cold that stopped me –

not from outside, not the weather. It was the ice inside me that meant I couldn't cry.

I was tired, though. I kept my eyes open for most of the evening, I think. I didn't look at my watch because it was too cold to raise my hand, but I knew it was late because of the absence of cars and the disappearing lights from the nearby houses. Later, much later I think, I heard an owl hooting eerily in the dark. I must have fallen asleep eventually, my head on the cold earth, my knees up to my chest.

They found me like that the next morning. Some kids were making a detour on their way to school, using their boots to stamp on the ice puddles and making clouds with their hot breath. They saw me curled up on the ground like a sleeping animal. At first they thought I was dead, and there was a great furore with mums rushing over and the nearby lollipop lady using her mobile to call 999.

The paramedic kneeled on the ground beside me and put his ear to my chest. He could only just hear my heart, he said, beating hesitantly against the frozen air.

I knew nothing of this. After eight years of pretending, I was at rest.

# SEVENTEEN

The nursery was particularly busy in the week before Christmas. My Aunt Rosie seemed rushed off her feet and looked as though she was doing mental arithmetic each time she put money into the cash register. After the slow months of the autumn there was the welcome sound of cars crunching over the gravel, their doors opening and closing as people got out to look at the rows of newly-delivered Christmas trees. While we watched and waited for people to make their choices my Aunt Rosie and I stayed in the warmth of the nursery shop, putting together arrangements of holly for door wreaths and table decorations.

"You're not feeling too tired, are you?" Rosie said, her fingers working nimbly at the stalks of holly, her knitting needles lying idle in the living room.

I was feeling fine. She, on the other hand, was looking a touch harassed. My Uncle Jeff's van had broken down that morning on the way back from the wholesalers and was sitting in a layby a few kilometres away, waiting for the rescue services to come and fix it.

"Imagine that," Rosie had said, trying to make light of it. "With two dozen trees in the back the repair man will expect to see Father Christmas stepping out."

She giggled a little at this. I smiled politely. My Aunt

Rosie had taken to making little jokes. I knew she was trying to be cheerful, probably for my sake. As well as this she had bought herself some new clothes for my visit: large floral shirts and cotton trousers with trainers. She'd taken to wearing long, dramatic earrings that danced about as she bustled around. It was a new image, quite unlike her dresses and skirts and green Wellingtons. At first I wasn't sure why she had adopted it. Then, a day or two into my visit, I realized: she was trying to be like a friend to me. She was trying to dress younger and be more of a pal than an aunt. I felt immediately touched by this. There was no need for her to worry about me. I was not unhappy. In fact I felt more relaxed than I had been for years.

My Uncle Jeff still looked just the same: a green zip-up jacket, checked shirt, jeans and boots. It was a uniform that he'd been wearing for years, occasionally adding a peaked cap if it was too sunny or a woolly hat if it was particularly cold. His mood, though, was different. He seemed out of sorts and a little tense.

"He's got some things on his mind. Then there's the Christmas rush," Rosie said. "We must have had at least, let me see, at least *ten* customers in this morning. It's like the first day at the Harrods sale!"

And she giggled again, her fingers working deftly at a holly wreath, its berries like red beads among the sharp green leaves. An hour or so later, my uncle arrived in his van, parked at an untidy angle and started to unload the Christmas trees. Rosie left me on my own and went out to talk to him. I couldn't hear their words but the tone was unmistakably terse. I wondered if he was annoyed at my presence. I'd been there over a week and there was still almost a week to go until Christmas.

"It's nothing to do with you," Rosie said later, handing me a mug of steaming tea. "He's just worried about the new garden centre."

She showed me the article in their local paper about the giant supermarket development. It was to be a couple of kilometres down the road, in the middle of the disused airfield on which Rosie had suggested we practise driving. Part of it was definitely going to be a garden centre.

"Will it go ahead, do you think?" I said.

"If it does it will close us down," Rosie said, turning at the sound of another car coming into the drive. She put the newspaper down by the till and rushed out.

I didn't see that much of Jeff anyway. He seemed to spend most of his time toing and froing between the wholesalers and the nursery. When he wasn't driving round he was taking care of the stock. In the evening he worked in the nursery office, or sat in the dining room listening to music and doing crosswords with his fountain pen. Beside him there was often a bottle of whisky and next to it a glass the size of an eggcup. He often gave me a weary smile and read out a difficult clue. I hardly ever knew the answer. He toasted me anyway and went back to his paper.

I spent most of my time with Rosie: working,

shopping, watching television, cooking and even, once or twice, sitting in the driver's seat of her car, moving forwards and backwards around the nursery paths.

It was almost four weeks since the night in Sparrow Gardens, and I had physically recovered. Rosie was still treating me with great care, making me frequent cups of tea and fussing over me. Some of the time I sat next to the cash register in the nursery shop, taking the money for the trees, a small two-bar electric fire by my side, singeing my ankles and keeping me far warmer than was necessary. When it was quiet I would walk back into the giant greenhouse, tending to the rows of potted poinsettias, their giant red flowers brazen and beautiful. I had to pack them into plastic trays, getting them ready for the trip to several markets in the days that led up to Christmas. I was busy and I liked it.

I didn't miss being at college, although I did miss being at home. My mum and dad rang every day and they were coming to take me home on Christmas Eve. Rosie had a full timetable for me up to then.

When they found me I was very cold. Someone said I'd been suffering from suspected hypothermia. The paramedics had taken me straight to hospital and I'd been slowly warmed up. I don't remember much about it, but I had this picture in my head of myself like a block of ice slowly defrosting, water dripping from the corners on to the floor, my mum and dad standing beside me wearing layers and layers of clothes, hats and gloves.

There were questions, of course: the nurses, the doctors and the police. Only my mum and dad didn't ask anything. They knew why I hadn't been able to go home. They knew and they were going to make it all right. They took me home and put me to bed for days, bringing trays of soup and tempting food up to my room. My mum sat by my bed in her jeans and sweatshirt and told me over and over not to worry, that I hadn't done anything wrong, that in their grief over Judy they'd forgotten that I too was a child and that they'd almost lost me as well.

It was a confusing few weeks. I'd watched television mostly, letting the talk shows fill my bedroom with chatter. From downstairs I heard the front-door bell going and voices of visitors – the police probably, I thought. My mum had told them about the red van, I knew that much. They had moved on, though, with the search of the house in Willow Drive. The red van was no longer important to them.

Although there was lots of concern for me, from my mum and dad, Rosie and Jeff, Clare from college (even a number of text messages from Teresa Russell), I actually felt better than I had for a long time. The truth about my lie was out. The story about the American girl was out. I had thrown it all up in the air for other people to catch. I felt lightheaded with relief.

The American woman from Willow Drive was not the same as my American woman. The police contacted Ann Carter after they'd done the forensic tests. She was living in Alabama with her husband and two children.

She told them what she knew about the house and the man who had stayed there with her. His name was Tom Banner and he had been a student, like her, but had dropped out of college. He'd helped to lay the garden paving stones, she'd said, as a way of repaying back rent. The police were looking for him, Rosie told me. He was the closest thing they had to a suspect.

This was all I knew and all I wanted to know. I felt like I was floating on calm waters after being in a choppy sea. In the background the investigation was still going on, like a train travelling on a distant line, its noise like an echo in my ear. My mum and dad were creeping round trying to keep it all from me. I could hear their whispered phone calls from the office next door and the sound of the front door being shut quietly, letting the police or people from CHILDLOSS in or out.

When Rosie reminded me of her invitation to come and stay with them I said yes immediately. On the evening before I was due to go I went up to the computer and logged on to the email. There was a message for me from Shelly. I hesitated before opening it. I still felt awkward about the whole thing. Weeks before, I had fallen hungrily on to the information Shelly had sent. I had needed it. It had kept me going, but ultimately it had been hollow and I had been left starving and in worse condition than before. Now I was embarrassed at my neediness and the words One new message and the name Shelly made me cringe.

I opened the email anyway.

Dear Kim,

I'm sorry to hear you've been unwell. Your mom had a long conversation with mine a few days ago and I'm not really supposed to get in touch with you again. I guess this is a way of saying goodbye. Margaret and Judy left about a week ago. I was up early so I saw the storage company trailer picking up all their stuff. Beside it was a Winnebago (this is a kind of touring home, you have caravans in England, I think). Margaret told my mom that she had been offered a new contract by a company in Florida and she and Judy were going to spend three months driving coast-to-coast sightseeing. I watched from my bedroom window as they came out and Margaret locked up the house. She put the keys underneath the door and she and Judy headed for the Winnebago. Just before Judy got in she looked round and gave me a wave. She was a sweet kid and I'm sorry she didn't turn out to be your sister. Anyway, that's not the end of the story. A day or so after Margaret left the debt collectors arrived. She owed a lot of money, apparently. They knocked on our door and asked us if we had a forwarding address but we didn't. That's not all. Another one of our neighbours said there had been a private detective hanging around over the last couple of weeks asking questions about her. The rumour is that she was on the run from a violent husband, that Judy wasn't her adopted English daughter at all, but her own child, and she just assumed this new identity to get away from him. Then, yesterday, my mom heard a completely different story from the doctor's secretary (who is a friend from her book circle). She said that Margaret had been working for the FBI as an undercover agent in the pharmaceuticals industry and her cover had been blown (not by me, but at work). So which is true? No one knows. This morning I got a postcard from Judy. It's written in very scruffy handwriting so I'm guessing she did it secretly. It's from Las Vegas and she said that they're having a great time and that she misses me and all her friends in Seattle. So that's it. Margaret and Judy might not be connected to you but they're still a mystery. I hope you're feeling a lot better and that you have some news about your sister soon. Lots and lots of love.

Your dear American friend Shelly

I folded the email up and thought about the girl, Judy, walking through the casinos in Las Vegas past rows of one-armed bandits and walls of sparkling neon lights. In my head I saw her with a giant cup of drink, the straw in her mouth, her arm loosely linked through Margaret's. I smiled at this. They were running away from something. A pair of fugitives. It gave the whole story a kind of romantic finish, and I suddenly felt easy with it.

The next day we drove to the nursery. It was drizzling, much warmer than it had been. It was the first time I'd been out for ages. The winding country lanes were wet and shiny, the car splashing lightly through surface water. I felt exhilarated, as if I was leaving all my troubles behind me. My mum gave me a bear hug and told me to save the best Christmas tree for them. I chose a large Norwegian Fir and stacked it in the back of the nursery.

Outside the nursery shop I watched as my Aunt Rosie

moved quickly from customer to customer. She came towards me, leading a man by the elbow. She was breathless, her pink flowered shirt billowing out behind, her pendulum earrings swinging back and forth.

"Kim, take this man's money, will you. We seem to have a bit of a rush out front."

I smiled at the man and took a twenty-pound note from him. Out of the window I could see three cars pulling up side by side, and my aunt fussing round, fluffing the branches of the trees out so that they looked their best. My Uncle Jeff was standing off to the side, leaning against the office door, his arms folded across his chest, his face glum. I gave the man a receipt and he left, heading for his car. The other customers were milling round, talking to Rosie, pointing at the trees.

I looked at the newspaper on the counter. The headline was just visible. **SUPERMARKET DEVELOPMENT WILL DESTROY LOCAL BUSINESSES.** Underneath there was a picture of an empty field with some crumbling buildings in the middle. Underneath the caption said, *Fairfax Aerodrome, last used 1972.*

I had to stop reading it, though, because my aunt was making hand signals to me. I picked up as many of the holly wreaths as I could and rushed out to the cars.

# EIGHTEEN

I didn't stop thinking about Judy in those days leading up to Christmas Eve. How could I? Before leaving home to go and stay at Rosie's my mum and me went up to the loft and looked through the box of family photographs. We picked out half a dozen photos of Judy, ranging from a baby shot to one that was taken the summer before she disappeared. On the back of each we wrote a caption: *A day at Southend; Picking flowers at the nursery; In Dad's new car; Playing rounders in the forest; With Toby; With Kim at her birthday party.*

These weren't the only things we took from the loft. Mum picked up an old cloth rabbit and a couple of the tiny figures from the doll's house. She also pulled out a book of Judy's that I hadn't seen for years and years. It was a story of a tomboy princess who hated all the princes who asked her to marry them. Judy loved it, especially when the princess turned them all into horrible frogs. I remembered reading it to her when she was about three, usually when she was in bed. It was one of many stories she insisted on before going to sleep. Often I was tired myself and tried to skip a page. She wouldn't have it, though, and I had to go back and read every single word and point out every bit of every picture.

I took all these things with me to Rosie and Jeff's and put them on my bedside table. Every morning when I woke up I allowed myself a little time to look through them and think about Judy. It was something Pam had suggested and I had finally got round to taking her advice. The memories no longer upset me as they had done before. Since the truth had come out I felt easier with my thoughts about Judy. I even enjoyed them in a funny sort of way.

A couple of days before Christmas Eve, while I was in the bathroom washing my hair, I could hear Rosie calling me. She must have realized where I was, because when I went back into my room she was there looking at the pictures of Judy.

"Sorry, I was looking for you and I saw these…" she said, looking embarrassed. "You've got a visitor. Clare? She's in the kitchen."

"Oh," I said, pleasantly surprised.

I towel-dried my hair and went downstairs to find Clare eating toast. Rosie had taken a posh china teapot out and was spooning tea from a canister into it.

"Your aunt's making me Earl Grey," Clare said.

"Nice to see you," I said, and meant it.

"I thought I'd come by and bring your present," she said, brightly.

In front of her there was a small parcel wrapped in bright red paper. Around it there was silver ribbon tied into a flamboyant bow in the middle. I felt immediately guilty. I hadn't bought anything for her.

"Come on," she said, registering my expression. "You've not exactly been up to going out shopping. Anyway, I didn't buy this. I made it!"

I took the small parcel from her and felt around it for a moment. I was moved, particularly at the ornate bow which had been so carefully tied. Rosie poured Clare's tea out into a china mug and stood looking at the present.

"Go on, open it," Clare said, stabbing a long finger at it. "It's only three days to Christmas, after all."

I noticed that her fingernails had speckles of red paint on them and the skin on her hands had a greenish tinge. I imagined she'd been painting some kind of Christmas theme. I was sure it wouldn't be a traditional greetings-card type of picture.

"I'll be out in the nursery," Rosie said, leaving us on our own.

Inside the red paper was a small wooden box. It was about the size of a paperback book. The lid of it was intricately painted with floral designs.

"Did you make this?" I said, lifting the lid.

"No, I lied about that. I did paint it though. It's for small things: pieces of jewellery, chains, earrings and stuff."

I couldn't say anything. For an awful moment I thought I might cry, so I forced myself to laugh instead.

"It's brilliant. Thanks so much."

I reached out and gave her hand a squeeze. Her fingers felt dry and gritty from the paint and clay that she handled all day and every day. She put her other hand on top of mine and I felt the warmth of her grasp. For a moment I felt as though I would burst with gratitude. I wanted to laugh at the silliness. It was only a box with painted flowers on the lid, but I wasn't used to such simple affection. It had been a long time since I'd had a proper friend.

I walked her back to her car a little later.

"Have you been thinking much about the American girl?" she said.

I nodded. I'd told her all about it when I was still at home, after the night in Sparrow Park. She'd not been as dismissive as I'd expected. She'd listened wide-eyed and seemed to feel that I hadn't been that silly to think that the American Judy and my sister might be the same person. She'd asked dozens of questions and looked enthusiastically at the emails and the photographs. She'd gone off home that night with an excited twitch about her shoulders, and I half expected to see some paintings about fractured families or hands across the sea.

"I should push it out of my mind," I said. "I mean, I know she's not my Judy. I know that now. But I kept thinking about her. Walking along a street in some American city, wearing sneakers and chewing bubblegum. You know, a stereotype American teen. I just can't seem to get that image out of my head."

"Is that such a bad thing?" Clare said.

"But she's not my sister. Trouble is, now, when I think

about *my* Judy, I visualize the face of this American girl. It's like they're mixed up somewhere in my head."

I was stumbling over my words because I hadn't really worked out what I was saying. To tell the absolute truth, I hadn't really known I felt that way until I said it.

"This American girl? She's on a journey somewhere, isn't she?" Clare said, looking thoughtful.

I nodded.

"Why not think of her when you think of Judy? It's what she might have been like if she had lived."

I was taken aback. *If she had lived*. Clare had said it with honesty. She had used words that were almost never uttered.

"In America?" I said, weakly.

"Why not? If that makes you feel good. Think of this American girl as a kind of symbol of your sister. A free spirit, travelling somewhere. Enjoying life. Just because someone snatched her away from you eight years ago, it doesn't mean you can't take some pleasure in what her life might have been like."

"Isn't that deluding myself?"

"No, not as long as you know, deep down, that it's not her. Just a facsimile of her. A kind of moving portrait. Look, for five years your sister led a happy life. If she'd grown up she might have been just like this American girl. Why shouldn't you think about that? Why should this man who took her also take away all those dreams you might have had about her? Don't let him do that. Use this American girl as a kind of composite teenager and think about her as your sister. Why not?"

I nodded. Clare's words were like balm, soothing, comforting. She was leaning on the driver's door of her car, the keys hanging from her little finger. She was so forthright about things. She just said what she thought. She had a way of ignoring all the difficult terrain and heading straight to the top of the mountain. I remembered then that I'd asked her almost nothing about her own life. I could have kicked myself.

"How's your mum's boyfriend and your dad?" I said.

"A bit better. They don't actually come to blows these days. They talk civilly when they meet. That's probably the most we can expect."

She got into her car and wound the window down.

"See you after Christmas? Back at college?"

I nodded. It was a sort of plan I had. I waved at her as she drove out of the nursery gates. I stood still for a few minutes. I felt good and was thinking about what she'd said, picturing the American Judy standing beside a Christmas tree in her quilted zipper jacket. I was about to turn and walk back into the house when another car turned into the car park. It was an ordinary make with a man at the wheel and a woman sitting beside him. They parked in a leisurely way, the woman got out and the man stayed where he was for a moment, talking on a mobile phone. She was wearing a smartish mac over trousers and he was wearing a suit. There was nothing odd or unusual about them and the man was friendly when he asked me if the owners were around.

It was something in their walk, or the confidence with which they spoke, that gave them away. They were plain-clothes police officers. I pointed towards the back door of the house and watched them walk off. I took a step, half intending to follow them, but I changed my mind.

My previous good mood had evaporated, and I was left loitering by the side of a row of Christmas trees.

# NINETEEN

I was sure they had come to say that Judy's body had been found. I had no intention of going into the house after them, so I walked in the direction of the nursery shop. I went inside and closed the door. The fire wasn't on so I plugged it in and sat up on the high chair next to the counter and the cash register. From where I was sitting I could see across the yard to Rosie's back kitchen. They were all standing, my aunt and uncle and the two detectives. There was a conversation going on, and I could see heads nodding and hands moving and the mouths of my aunt and uncle opening and shutting.

Rosie wasn't making them any tea, and that was a bad sign. I felt myself sitting very still, my legs curled round each other, then looked down to see that I was clutching Clare's Christmas present tightly, as though it was some sort of life-line. I loosened my hold on the small wooden box and ran my fingers over the painted lid. I felt an awful foreboding. I stood up and walked around agitatedly. I placed Clare's box on my uncle's desk, next to his computer.

I sneaked a look back out of the window to see if there was any movement, but the four of them were standing in the same positions. It was like watching a film that had stuck on *pause*. I wanted to know why they were there; what it was they had come to talk about. I suppose I could have gone in with them. I was Judy's sister, I had every right to know any developments. But I couldn't have followed them in and listened to their bald words.

I was afraid. In my head, buried underneath the fantasies about the American girl, the vague hope that somewhere, somehow Judy was still alive, there was the certain knowledge that one day Judy's body would be found. At the same time as ignoring this possibility, I was also bracing myself for it.

The back kitchen door was opening and the four of them walked out into the car park. My aunt was first, marching towards the nursery shop, her shirt flying out behind her. She looked like she meant business. The detectives were standing talking to my uncle. They all seemed quite relaxed. I felt my shoulders drop and I swallowed a couple of times, noticing how dry my mouth was. The woman looked up at the sky and put her hand out as if she was saying something about the weather. They were all glancing in the direction of the nursery shop and waiting for something.

"You won't believe it," my aunt said, bursting through the shop door.

I looked expectantly at her, rubbing at the tops of my arms where my muscles felt tight.

"This man that they're questioning, this Tom Banner, he says that the paving stones were laid by our company."

I frowned. I was lost for a minute, I didn't know what

she was talking about. She had stepped past my uncle's desk to the filing cabinet and was bending down and pulling open the bottom drawer. She was a bit puffed, I could tell. I looked out of the window at the male police officer who was talking to Jeff. My uncle was zipping his jacket up and downand looked as though he was listening hard to something. The woman had walked off and was looking at the Christmas trees.

"We keep our old records in this bottom drawer. I know eight years is a long time, but you just never know when the tax people are going to query something. Where is it? Here ... look, you wouldn't believe it…"

She pulled a file out of the drawer and plonked it on the desk.

"I don't understand," I said.

"This man they're questioning, you know the one who shared the house with the American woman?"

She coughed lightly at this as though she didn't actually want to mention the *American* woman in case it upset me.

"They've found him?" I said.

"A couple of days ago. Turns out he's one of these New Age Travellers. That's why it took them so long to track him down. He'd taken on a new name and was living in some camp near Wales. He's denying everything of course. He's saying he didn't even lay that particular bit of the garden. He says he was helping some old boy called Frank Lewis who worked for us—"

"He remembered the nursery?" I said.

She had the folder open on the desk and was flicking through a pile of papers.

"No, he remembered Frank and where he lived. It was Frank's wife who told the police about us."

"Oh."

It was an odd turn of events. Rosie saw my face and stopped what she was doing for a moment. Her voice softened.

"You remember, when Judy went missing, me and Jeff we spent a lot of time over your house? And then with the miscarriage... Well, Jeff and me ... we weren't fit to run any business. No, in those weeks after it all happened Frank Lewis ran things. He must have supplied the paving stones and got a few quid for helping with the job."

She turned back and began sorting through the papers again.

"Here," she said, suddenly, and held up a piece of paper.

I looked at it. The nursery heading was printed on it but the receipt was in handwriting. It had the address in Willow Drive and then the amount of stones. There was no mention of any payment for the work.

"Look at the date," Rosie said, in a half whisper.

It was three days after Judy disappeared. Rosie turned and walked out of the shop and marched back towards the officers. All of them, my uncle and the man and woman, peered at the receipt. There was some head-shaking, and some comments. Nobody looked happy or angry, surprised or upset. The police officers left soon after, taking the receipt with them. My uncle watched the car disappear and then he turned and went into the house. My aunt came back into the shop.

"That's an unpleasant development," she said, thoughtfully. "To think we might have provided the paving stones... I should think poor Frank would turn in his grave."

She stopped speaking, looking out of the shop window at the empty car park. I could tell she was thinking hard because her eyes were moving about and she was knitting her fingers together. I looked down at the desk where the old folder was still open, the piles of papers in it askew. I put my hand in to tidy them up, and my fingers touched on something. I pulled out a photograph. When I turned it over I found myself looking at a picture of my sister and me outside the nursery shop on a hot summer's day. Rosie saw me looking at it.

It had been taken eight years before and we were both in our best clothes. Two little girls looking at the camera, my sister's dimples and her curly hair making her look like a doll. By the side of her I looked long-faced, my hair straight and my smile a little crooked. Behind her was my Uncle Jeff, sitting on a chair next to another much older man, with a mop of white hair.

I remembered the photograph. My uncle had put it in a small silver frame and placed it on the wall above the till in the nursery shop. *His lovely nieces*, he'd said.

"That's Frank Lewis," Rosie said. "Do you remember him?"

"Not really. Not that well."

"He was over sixty then. He was a retired farm worker who Jeff met down at the pub. He used to help us out in busy times, spring and summer. We gave him his wages in cash so he didn't have to pay tax. He was a lovely man. Really good with children. He sometimes used to bring his own grandchildren over. He loved you and Judy. I think you were a bit shy but Judy was always chatting to him."

Rosie's face had a contented look, as though she had transported herself back eight years and was sitting in the sunshine with Judy and me and Jeff and Frank Lewis.

"He was only sixty-two when he had a heart attack."

She placed the photograph up against the cash register and tidied away the old folder.

"How awful to think that Frank might have helped lay the paving stones in that garden..." she said.

I didn't want to think about that. I looked closely at the picture of my sister and noticed that she was wearing her gold neck-chain, her fingers holding the "J" out as though showing it to someone. At least she wasn't sucking on it. I thought of the other Judy and the "J" that she wore round her neck. I imagined her fiddling with it as she sat in her classroom at school, lounging in one of those funny chair-desks that the Americans use.

From behind me I could hear the sounds of a car

pulling in to the nursery car park. I looked out and saw a couple and their children getting out of a Land Rover, a small boy running excitedly towards the Christmas trees, the girl, a little older, hanging back, looking fed-up with the whole trip. I pushed the photograph across the counter to Rosie, who seemed to be in a world of her own. Then I went out to see if I could sell another Christmas tree.

# NINETEEN

That evening my aunt and uncle had a row. I had gone to bed about eleven and tried to go to sleep. After a while of tossing and turning I decided to get up and make myself a cup of tea. I'd assumed that Rosie and Jeff had gone to bed so I ran downstairs in my nightdress and bare feet. The radiators had gone off and it felt cold. I regretted not wearing my slippers, especially on the stone floor in the kitchen.

It all took longer because my aunt didn't have any tea bags and I had to spoon the tea into a tiny teapot and let it sit for a few moments. I noticed their voices then, from across the hall in the living room. The kitchen clock showed that it was past midnight. I was surprised. They were usually tucked up in bed before me. Especially Jeff, who liked to make an early start most mornings.

I took the lid off the teapot and stirred. I heard my uncle's voice a little louder and the sound of my aunt shushing him. I couldn't help but listen for a few minutes.

"What does it matter if the new supermarket opens? We can sell up. It's not like we've been doing wonderful business ourselves."

There was a low murmur which I knew was Jeff.

"OK, so we'd lose money. That's not the end of the world! We've been talking about doing something different for years."

"Like going abroad?"

I heard my uncle's voice, sharp and quick, as though it was a phrase he'd used often.

"You know why we haven't been able to do that. How could I leave my sister at a time like—"

"It's been eight years," Jeff said, harder.

I began to feel uncomfortable. I picked up the teapot and filled my mug. I went to the fridge to get out the milk. I was tiptoeing, trying not to make a noise. I felt as though I shouldn't be there, a witness to their argument. I closed the fridge door as quietly as I could. I picked up my cup and just then I heard the living-room door open and the voices get louder. I dithered. I could have just walked out into the hall and let them see I was there. It wouldn't have been so very embarrassing. All married couples have rows. I'd heard my mum and dad often enough. But something stopped me. This didn't sound like an everyday argument about how much money they had in their bank account.

"Look," Rosie's voice softened, "maybe this new superstore won't hurt us as much as we think it will. We have loyal customers..."

"Don't be ridiculous. There's no such thing as loyalty where money is concerned. We buy a hundred pots, the store will buy ten thousand. Of course they can sell them at two-thirds of the price that we can. We're finished."

"There's the expertise," my aunt rushed on. "These stores, they're full of teenagers serving behind tills. We've got the know-how. We can give advice. We could specialize: patio gardens, water features, organic flowers. There's all sorts of things…"

"We could have gone away. Five years ago we could have bought into that nursery in Spain. It would have been a fresh start for us. Away from here. Away from all this…"

My Uncle Jeff sounded close to tears.

"I couldn't go. I couldn't leave my sister…"

"She has her own family. She still has Kim!"

"She needed me… Oh, I don't know how you can argue at a time like this. For goodness' sake! We could be close to finding Judy! How can you be so cold? What does it matter if a supermarket opens and we lose our business? Look at what my sister lost!"

"We lost something too," Jeff said, quick as a flash. "We lost our baby."

"I had a miscarriage. How can you possibly compare that to what my sister went through?"

I found myself backing into the corner, afraid that one of them would walk across and come into the kitchen. I didn't want to have to face them in the middle of such a raw argument.

"We lost our baby."

I noticed then that Jeff's voice sounded slurred.

"We would have probably lost the baby whatever. These things happen. My miscarriage may have had

161

nothing to do with what happened to Judy."

"No, Rosie. Everything in our lives has something to do with your sister's family. Our lives together, our home, our business, our bank balance…"

"Perhaps our bank balance might be healthier if you drank less of that stuff," my aunt bounced back. "Perhaps we wouldn't be so worried then about the supermarket."

"We could have gone anywhere. We had no ties. We could have travelled the world!"

"I couldn't… Not with Judy…"

"So how long will it be before we can live our own lives? Ten years? Twenty years? How long before we can get over it?"

"But that's it. You've just made my point. There is no getting over it. This thing … that happened to my sister, it affected us all. Oh, Kim and Maureen and Roger most of all, but then me and then you and then friends and neighbours. It affected everyone."

"But everyone else went back to living their own lives."

There was a hiccupping sound and I knew my aunt was crying. In my hand was a mug of lukewarm tea and my legs and feet felt numb with cold. Then I heard my uncle's voice.

"I'm sorry, Rosie. Please don't cry. I'm just upset about this damn store down the road. I don't blame you for standing by Maureen. I understand."

I heard footsteps then and snuffles as my aunt went upstairs. My uncle's voice followed her up. "It's my fault.

I'm just stressed because of the business. You're right, I do drink too much…"

I let them go and stood there for a full five minutes. I poured my tea into the sink and crept upstairs and into my room. I got under the duvet and wrapped it round my legs and feet and thought about my aunt and uncle and the past eight years. They'd always been there for my mum and dad; they were solid and dependable and, in the early days, optimistic. At first my aunt had been sure that Judy would come back. She thought that some sad childless woman had Judy and was looking after her and would, in due course, return her. When that didn't happen she seemed shaken, and spent her time in the kitchen making meals that no one wanted. My Uncle Jeff always seemed to have a glass in his hand and was constantly offering my mum or dad a brandy.

Then Rosie miscarried. She was sixteen weeks pregnant and the doctor told her it had been a girl. It was terrible for her, but she played it down. Like a light shower after a hurricane, it went unnoticed, hardly commented on. At the time I hadn't given it a moment's thought. I don't think any of us had.

That night I lay in my aunt's spare bedroom, curled up in her duvet, and thought how different things would have been if the baby had lived.

Both of them, my mum and my aunt, lost a child that terrible year.

# TWENTY

At breakfast the next morning Rosie was humming cheerfully. Even though it had gone nine o'clock I was still rubbing the sleep from my eyes. The kitchen was warm and filled with the smell of baking. On the work-surface was a layer of rolled-out pastry and a jar of mincemeat. Rosie was looking very festive in a bright-red shirt over some newish denim jeans that had had a crease ironed into them. She had dangling Christmas tree earrings on and I thought, for a moment, that they were flashing on and off.

"Tea?" she said, brightly.

I nodded and looked out of the window to see my uncle loading up the van with trays of poinsettias. With only two shopping days to go before Christmas he had a lot to do. I pulled a chair out and sat down, wondering if I should rush upstairs and get dressed so that I could help him. Rosie placed a mug of steaming tea in front of me and then turned back towards the pastry.

"Thought I'd do a couple of trays of mince tarts for you to take home tomorrow. Your dad loves these and the shop-bought ones just aren't the same."

I wasn't really listening, just trying to drink my tea, blowing the steam out of the way before gingerly sipping. Just then I noticed a familiar car sweeping past my uncle's van and parking. The was a squeal from the tyres as the brakes were applied. It made me jump a little and I put my mug down and sat up. It was my mum's car. Jeff turned and walked towards her just as she got out. She put her arm on his and beckoned to him to come into the house. My dad wasn't with her and she looked flustered, her shirt collar jutting untidily out of a zip-up jacket that was hanging loose. She didn't seem to have a bag or a case. She wasn't holding anything except her bunch of car keys. Her face was pale and her hair hadn't been combed. Something had happened, I knew.

Rosie saw my intent stare and looked out the window.

"Oh lor'!" she said, clapping her hands together so that little clouds of flour floated in the air. I had a sudden memory of that night at Teresa's, the three of us making jam tarts. Rolling the pastry out until it was the thickness of a pound coin, using the templates to make heart shapes and circles, spooning the jam, as red as blood, on to the tarts.

I stood up when my mum came in, followed by Jeff. I put my hand out to her but she hardly noticed me. Her arm was as stiff as a board and I could feel the cold radiating off her skin.

"The police rang this morning," she said.

Rosie gripped on to the chair in front of her.

"Have they found…"

"No, no." My mum shook her head vehemently. "No, not yet. It's about Frank. They phoned me about Frank Lewis."

"What about Frank?" Jeff asked.

"It seems… I'm sure you didn't know. How could you? Otherwise you would never have let him near the girls…"

"What? What?" Jeff said, shaking my mum's arm.

"The police said that he has something on his record. An assault. When he was fifty, a neighbour's child said that he … assaulted her."

"You mean he hit her? Not Frank," Rosie said, her voice a little louder, trying to be firm.

"No, not that sort of assault. He touched her… Sexual assault…"

"No," Jeff shook his head, "no, not Frank *Lewis*. I don't believe it."

He enunciated the surname, his head shaking, his mouth pulled into a straight line.

"It seems it wasn't proved. Never tested in court. His name just stayed on their records and there was never anything else. The police contacted the girl – well, young woman now, she's in her early twenties. She insists that he did touch her."

"I can't understand…"

"The police say that Tom Banner isn't budging on his story. And there's no forensic evidence to link him with any of Judy's clothes. Now they're looking at Frank Lewis. They're saying maybe he was driving past when Judy was walking along Willow Drive."

We all stood very still.

"Judy knew him, you see. If he stopped and opened

the car door, she would have seen a friendly face, someone she knew. He wasn't a *stranger*."

My mum seemed to stumble for a moment and then leaned on the table. Rosie came round and pulled a chair out so that she could sit on it. I leaned over and put my hand on my mum's shoulder. There was the slightest of trembles, as though she was holding everything in.

"The police are going to search the house he lived in with his wife. They also want to search the nursery grounds."

Jeff's face was waxen and Rosie put her hands up to her mouth.

"The police think that Judy could be ... here?" Jeff said.

"Not necessarily. They don't know. They're still looking for the rest of her clothes..." My mum held the palms of her hands up in resignation.

"What about Frank's wife and family?" Jeff said.

Rosie looked at him with dismay.

"What about them?" she said, her tone strident.

"I can't believe that Frank... I knew him for years. There was no sign. No suggestion. He was just an ordinary family man. What's his wife going to say?"

"What does it matter?" Rosie said, exasperated.

"I should go over and see her..."

"Why?"

But Jeff had walked out, muttering something under his breath. I watched as he went across the car park to his van. His shoulders were rounded and his head was down. He opened the door of the van and drove off in seconds. Rosie had pulled a chair over and was sitting with my mum, her back to the window and the car park.

I put the kettle on and waited for the water to boil while my mum and Rosie talked. I thought of the photo of Frank Lewis, the nice man who worked in the nursery during their busy times, and Judy standing next to him chatting. Since the previous day my memory of him had become more substantial. I did recall his presence in the nursery shop. A solid man with wiry white hair and a red face. He always had a tin of tobacco with him and a small packet of cigarette papers, and whenever things were quiet he would roll himself a couple of cigarettes. Judy always watched in fascination and kept asking if she could make one. *More than my life's worth*, he'd say, tutting. My Aunt Rosie had said that I was a little shy of him, but that wasn't true. There was a heavy smell about him that I didn't like. At the time I didn't know what it was, but my mum said he always had a bag of aniseed drops on him, so I thought it was that.

I made the tea, letting it brew in the pot and putting out three mugs. Rosie seemed near to tears.

"Poor Rosie," my mum said. "The police say they probably won't search the nursery grounds until after the Christmas break. But you don't want to be here now. You and Jeff must come and stay with us for Christmas. Come today, tonight, whenever you're ready. I'll take Kim with me now, and you and Jeff come over when you're ready."

Rosie was nodding her head stiffly, her lips pressed together.

I felt a shiver of annoyance that I couldn't dismiss. I had come to the nursery to be with my aunt and uncle, and to get away from Judy, but she had followed me there. My sister and her story had pursued me. When she was alive she'd always been hanging round me, wanting to talk, wanting to play, wanting to be with me and be my best friend. Now that she was dead her memory clung on to everything I did, every place I went, every thought I had. Was that the way it would always be? Would it follow me everywhere? All my life? I found myself looking at the half-made mince tarts. I put my tea down and went over. I picked up the jar of mincemeat and started to spoon it neatly on to the tarts. All the time I could hear my mum and Rosie murmuring. I continued cutting out the pastry tops and covered the fillings. Would I ever be free of this thing that had happened to my family? Or would it sit like a heavy yoke around my neck for the rest of my life? I put my hands on the work-surface and pushed against it. There was a sense of injustice uncurling inside me, the beginnings of anger rearing its head. Why me? Why our family?

I thought about my dad. Where was he? With the police? At home on his own? In the office typing out a CHILDLOSS newsletter? Maybe he was out buying Christmas presents. I pictured him walking through a department store clutching several carrier bags, his face tired but happy. I found myself breathing shallowly, almost hearing the Christmassy music in the background, imagining myself there, in that shop, spending my money on presents, wishing I was not steeped in sorrow for a lost sister. For that moment I wished I'd never had a sister. I wished she'd never been born and then the rest of us would never have had such a miserable, heartbreaking time.

A great sob of guilt bubbled out of me. I stopped what I was doing and concentrated hard to hold it in. I found my fingers digging into the tray of mince tarts. There was a sudden silence from behind me. I knew that Rosie and my mum had stopped talking and were looking in my direction. I didn't turn round. I didn't run to them for comfort. I swallowed and swallowed until the tears had gone back to where they came from. Then I picked up the tray of tarts, took it over to the cooker and gently put it in the top shelf of the oven.

I stood back to wait for them to cook. This time they wouldn't burn, and then I would take them home as a treat for my dad.

# TWENTY ONE

Rosie and Jeff weren't due to arrive until late afternoon on Christmas Eve. They were delivering trees and plants and tidying up the loose ends in the nursery, Rosie had said. Then they would pack up their stuff and come over. My mum and dad and me threw ourselves into preparations for Christmas. We put up the Norwegian Fir tree and decorated it with tinsel and some new flashing lights my dad had bought a couple of days before.

"We want this to be a good Christmas," my mum said brightly.

Her cheerfulness was only a veneer, though, and I could see the worry lines at the corners of her mouth. Nevertheless, we went along with it. My dad was humming as he fiddled with the control panel of the lights. They flashed rapidly on and off or blinked slowly or stayed on all the time. He kept showing us each version and we stood back, like normal people in a normal family, our arms crossed, considering which one we liked best.

I got a phone call from Clare asking me how I was and wishing me a happy Christmas. *See you next term!* she said, and as I replaced the receiver I remembered the present she had bought me, the small wooden box whose lid she had carefully painted. I'd left it at the nursery. On my uncle's desk in the shop. I rang Rosie and asked her to pick it up for me and she said she would.

We had always celebrated Christmas, even that first year after Judy went missing. It was a muted affair, though, with a small tree and some tinsel. What had surprised us all was the Christmas cards. They seemed to come in sackfuls and at first we couldn't believe they were all for us. *The Hockney Family*, most of them said, and then care of the local newspaper. Some of them came via the police station and some had no address at all, just our surname and the area. They were sympathy messages, really, little expressions of hope or sorrow written in cards with Father Christmas or nativity scenes or snow-capped trees and cottages with smoke winding out of the chimneys.

We read them all. Every one. We even stuck some up around the room. They did give comfort in a funny way. It was as though many people were thinking of Judy at that time, not just us, the family. It was only weeks since she had gone, and I think we all had this idea that she would be back by Christmas. We had a sixth sense that nothing and no one could be so cruel as to keep a little girl away from her own family on Christmas Day. I think my mum and dad even bought her presents, although they kept them hidden away from the rest of us.

The second Christmas was probably the worst. The media had forgotten us and the search for Judy had been scaled down. She was a file on the police computer database and we got an occasional phone call from the detective in charge of the case. There were just the usual greetings cards, the tree put up and the family's presents scattered around. As the five of us started on our Christmas dinner I looked at the empty chair which had been pulled away from the table and stuck in an alcove. Just for a moment I thought I glimpsed her there, a silent presence, peeping round the corner, as our knives and forks clicked and scraped at our plates.

That afternoon, when my mum and me had finished the tree and were having a rest, I asked her about my aunt's miscarriage.

"I don't know why she and Jeff never had any more children," she said, quietly. "I always thought it might have had something to do with Judy."

I nodded. I'd known the answer to my question before I'd even uttered it. I'd remembered Jeff's pained voice during the row I'd overheard, *How long will it be before we can live our own lives?* It had affected everyone, Rosie had said. Like throwing a stone at a window, the cracks had spread wide, splintering the glass with sharp discordant lines. There was no repairing it.

Rosie arrived about four. She was on her own and I helped her carry her stuff in, loads of it. There were three carrier bags full of fruit and cakes and bottles of wine. There were two cardboard boxes of presents, plus a big hold-all full of her and Jeff's clothes. When we'd brought it all in I ran back out to the car for her knitting bag.

"Jeff's doing a few last-minute things. Then he's going

173

to follow on," she said breathlessly. "Honestly, he's been so busy. He's been in the office all day long!"

She and my mum went upstairs to unpack and I heard them talking rapidly all the way up, as though they hadn't seen each other for weeks. I went downstairs and found my dad in the living room. He rolled his eyes in the direction of the ceiling and shrugged his shoulders. I sat down on the sofa, picked up the TV remote and started to click across the channels. There was the usual array of pre-Christmas programmes, game shows, quizzes, cartoons and films. I left it on the news channel and pressed the mute button. On the screen there were only pictures of last-minute shoppers, world leaders speaking, policemen, the pope in Rome; all of it without sound, like a bizarre silent movie.

My dad was looking better. He had some new trainers on and had had a haircut. His skin was flushed as though he'd been exerting himself, as though he'd been active. This was good. He'd spent far too long sitting in that armchair wearing his bedroom slippers. I was about to remark on this when I noticed a familiar face on TV. It was Inspector Robinson or Robbins or Roberts – I could never remember which. He was being interviewed by someone. I glanced at my dad who was watching. I didn't know whether to turn the sound on or not. I was half waiting for him to tell me, but he didn't. He just rested back in the chair and watched the policeman, his mouth opening and shutting. I left the remote on the coffee table and sat back myself. A picture of Judy appeared in the corner of the screen as he was speaking. It was small, like a passport photo. Then there was some footage of the house in Willow Drive where her clothes had been dug up.

It was almost eerie, watching the television with no sound. From upstairs I could hear the murmuring voices of my mum and Rosie and the sound of footsteps and drawers and doors opening and shutting. In the living room, though, there was a church-like hush. The lights on the Christmas tree were blinking on and off, reflecting on the screen, and my dad and I watched without comment. The outside of a police station was shown with police cars driving in and out of a gate. Then a head-shot of a man came on to the screen, the kind of picture taken when someone was arrested, only there were no numbers underneath it. It was Frank Lewis, younger than when we had known him. There was only the slightest sound from my dad, an intake of breath, no more. I watched, knowing that the voice-over was giving details of Frank Lewis's possible involvement. Maybe they were asking for help from the public. At this late stage, on the day before Christmas, would anyone be listening and would anyone care?

The inspector reappeared and his mouth opened and shut a few times. A phone number appeared at the bottom of the screen. And then it was over and there was the weather girl standing by a map ready to speak. She had on a red hat with a white bobble on it and looked faintly ridiculous. After a few moments I turned

175

and looked at my dad.

"It'll be over soon, won't it?" I said. "They'll find Judy and then we'll know what really happened?"

He nodded, his face strained. "We can give her a decent funeral and say goodbye."

I clicked the TV remote off and the screen went dark. There was a sort of solemnity in the room, as though we'd just said something momentous. I wanted to go over to my dad and hug him tightly, but just then I heard footsteps on the stairs, heavy ones, and I knew it was Rosie. She came into the room carrying a number of festive parcels.

"Look at me, Father Christmas," she said, bending over to place the gifts under the tree. "Oh, Kim, here's your present from Clare. I almost forgot it. Jeff came running out of the office just as I was about to drive off."

I took the box from her.

"That's nice," my dad said. "Did Clare paint it?"

I nodded, holding it out for him to see. It felt heavier, somehow, and there was a rattle as though something was inside. I opened the lid to look and saw, to my surprise, an envelope there. At first I thought it was for me, I thought Clare had put a little note in that I hadn't noticed. But instantly I dismissed that because I knew I'd already looked inside the box, on the morning she'd given it to me. There was some tiny writing on it that I could barely read. And then I realized that it said *Rosie*.

"There's a letter for you here," I said.

Rosie didn't hear, though, because she was chattering on about some lights she and Jeff had bought the previous year which hadn't worked and they'd taken them back three times and they still hadn't worked. In the end they'd got their money refunded.

The envelope that the letter was in was almost the same size as the box. Almost a perfect fit. On the front of it was definitely the name *Rosie* and I ran my fingers across it, curious to know what it was doing in my box. I felt a number of bumps as though something was stuck underneath. I put my fingers in the side and prised the envelope out and handed it to Rosie.

"This is for you," I said, raising my voice a little to catch her attention.

I looked back and saw a brassy-looking chain in the corner of the box. It was a dirty orangey colour. I felt it with my fingers, puzzled as to what it was and how it got there. Using my nails I tried to pick up the thin chain. In the back of my head I was aware that my aunt was looking at the envelope and saying, *What's this? What on earth is this? It's Jeff's handwriting!*

As the chain lifted off the bottom of the box, I noticed the flat gold letter that was underneath. The letter "J". I held it up so that it swung gently from side to side. My dad looked at it and me, confused, not sure what it was I was holding up. I heard the envelope being torn open and my aunt tutting and saying, *What's this all about!*

It was my sister's chain. I turned the box over for some explanation as to how it got there; as though it had been some sort of magician's trick and I was trying to puzzle it out. I could hear the door open and my mum saying, *What's that?* to Rosie.

I felt a distant pounding in my head as I watched the dirty chain hang in the air, the letter "J" curling away from me. The last time I had seen it it had been round my sister's neck. I closed my eyes and felt this swooning feeling.

"What's that?"

My mum's voice cut through the darkness and I was almost afraid to look at her because I knew that in seconds she would recognize it. Behind her, I could hear the rustle of paper as my Aunt Rosie opened the letter. Then her words.

"Oh Lord," she said, in a breathy voice. "Oh my… Oh no… Not Jeff… No, please… Not Jeff."

But it was from him. And so was the neck chain.

# TWENTY TWO

The letter was long and detailed, and while we were waiting for the police we read it over and over. Rosie was distraught and disbelieving. My mum and dad were stunned. After a while they slumped on either side of my aunt and held her while she sobbed quietly, shuddering from time to time. I stood away from them, leaning on the wall, the back of the sofa, the window ledge, disorientated. It was still Christmas Eve and in the corner the tree sat under twinkling lights, the presents underneath bright and gay. It was all the same and yet everything was completely different, as though we were inhabiting some kind of parallel world. I had opened a Pandora's box of secrets which was going to change our lives for ever. The letter lay discarded on the coffee table and I reached over and picked it up, three pieces of paper in all, and read it for the third time.

My Dear Rosie,

This will be harder for you to read, perhaps, than it is for me to write. It will also be the last time you ever hear from me, because I am a coward and like all such people I will try and take the easy way out. Don't try to look for me. I beg that much of you.

It was me who picked Judy up on that street eight

years ago. How often I have wanted to say those words out loud, to unburden myself of the terrible thing that happened that night. Instead I pushed them down and tried to cover up as best I could. Perhaps I was naïve to think that it would all die down and I would be able to live on as though it never happened. But I did. I should have spoken up at the time. I'll try to explain why I didn't. All I ask is that you read my story and don't completely hate me.

That November afternoon I was delivering supplies to some local outlets. I don't know if you remember anything about that time (other than poor Judy), but we weren't doing well. It had been a wet, dismal summer and we'd only shifted about sixty per cent of our stock. You were pregnant and I'd been hoping for good profits so that we could give our baby a good start. But the bank manager wasn't sympathetic, and there was talk about repossessing the house and business. I didn't tell you about it because I didn't want to worry you. I started drinking a lot. You probably noticed that at the time. What you didn't know was that I went into a pub most lunchtimes and had several drinks. And yes, I drove the van.

That afternoon I'd been late with some of the deliveries and one of the shops I did business with told me that they'd found another supplier. I was upset and I went back to the pub about four-ish. I had a couple of pints and set off for home about five-thirty. I was driving along a road that was near to Maureen and Roger's and that's when I saw little Judy, walking along. She had her pink top on and it stood out in the dark street. I pulled up. It was a cold night and she didn't even have a proper coat on. And she was on her own. I opened the door and she got in. She was half in tears about some balloon she'd had that had floated away and got caught in a tree. I soothed her down a bit. I think I promised I'd buy her another one. I do remember that I intended to drive her straight home.

Only I didn't. She said that her mum was out and her dad was in the shop. I tried her mum's mobile but it was switched off. I tried her dad's shop but there was no answer. I didn't know what to do so I thought I'd drive her to the nursery, ring her mum or dad when I got there. Then you and me could have taken her back later.

The accident happened on that dark stretch of road just off the dual carriageway. No other car was involved, I just took a bend too quickly. One minute I remember Judy chatting on, talking nineteen to the dozen, and the next I seemed to lose control of the steering wheel and the van veered off the road and into a hedge. I did put my foot on the brakes but the wheels were skidding and that only made it worse.

I blacked out for a few minutes or seconds, I don't know which. When I opened my eyes I was sitting, upright in my seat, my seat belt clamping me tightly back. The windscreen was intact and I wasn't injured. I felt dazed and kept blinking and trying to get my bearings. The accident itself and the time before it had momentarily gone from my mind, and all I knew was that I had been involved in something and I hadn't been hurt. Added to that no other car had been involved and the police were nowhere to be seen. I felt this huge sense of relief, and I even reached across to try the ignition and see if the van would start. It did.

I remembered Judy then. I turned, and saw her slumped like a ragdoll in her seat, her head lolling against the passenger window. The sight of her was a shock. I felt weak as water and I wanted to be sick. I had to get out of the van and go over to the ditch. My head was spinning, with the drink, I suppose. I walked back to the passenger door and opened it gently.

I realized then that she had no seat belt on. I hadn't told her to put it on, you see. I hadn't remembered. She'd climbed into my van and talked about her balloon and I'd just driven off without reminding her.

She was dead then. I knew that. I took her out of the car. There was blood on the side of her head and on her clothes and a shoe. She was still warm, though, and I tried to give her mouth-to-mouth even though I knew it was no use. I hugged her tightly. I would have done anything in the world to save her. I beg you to believe that.

I don't think she knew anything. One minute we were driving along and then we skidded round the corner. The momentum of the van must have flung her forward so that she hit the windscreen. It just killed her, I think. There was some blood but that was from a superficial cut. The injury that killed her must have been deeper –

skull fracture, brain haemorrhage. I don't know, I'm not a doctor.

I remember looking at the windscreen, running my fingers across it to see if there was a crack or any mark of impact. But there was nothing. She was such a tiny thing that she never even made a mark. I did find her chain. It must have come off, or perhaps she'd been holding it in her hands.

I laid her in the back of the van. I intended to go straight to a hospital but somehow I just ended up driving around. I was in a kind of daze and I ended up on the old aerodrome. I must have known or sensed that it was the sort of place where I was unlikely to meet anyone.

I stayed with her for hours. Then I left her there and went home. The next day, while you and the others were with the police, I went back and buried her. I kept her clothes and her shoe because they were stained with blood. I don't know what I intended to do with them. I went into a state of frozen emotion. It must have taken about a week to wear off and when it did I was almost hysterical with grief and guilt. And I was afraid. Every time I looked at her things I got into a panic.

So I buried them under some paving stones in a garden that Frank Lewis was working on. I don't know why I kept the chain. I can't explain it.

I am sorrier than you will ever know.

I beg you to forgive me. I know I don't deserve it.

Jeff

The door bell sounded and I thought it was the inspector. My mum and dad and Rosie were fused together on the sofa so I walked out to the front door, holding the letter, ready to hand it over.

But it was a group of carol-singers. Three teenage girls and a younger boy. They were a bit giggly, but then they started to sing. *Away in a Manger.* It was slightly off-key but once they got going it sounded nice. I let them sing on even though I could see, in the distance, a police car coming up the street and towards our house.

They sang a couple of verses and I stood transfixed. I didn't want them to stop.

# TWENTY THREE

The funeral was at the beginning of February. It was a bright, sharp day where the frost crunched underfoot and the sky was a deep Mediterranean blue. The cars came about ten, and me, my mum and dad and Rosie sat in the first one. In front of us was the hearse with Judy's white coffin covered in flowers.

In the car behind were other family members and some of the police who had worked on the case for so long. There were neighbours and friends as well as Judy's teacher from her primary school and some pupils.

The crematorium seemed full. There were many faces that I didn't recognize. And some that I did. Teresa Russell was there with her mum, and Clare had come with her mum and dad (at least, it could have been her dad, or her mum's boyfriend). Pam, my counsellor, was at the back and she waved to me.

The service was short and non-religious. A woman called Rosemary from the Humane Society, who we'd got to know in the weeks leading up to the funeral, acted as a sort of chairperson. She introduced it and spoke about Judy's life, telling stories that she'd learned from us. She talked about Judy's personality and her habits, her love of clothes and how she helped her dad in the baker's shop.

She didn't mention my Uncle Jeff. Why should she?

The police found him on Boxing Day, in his car, near the cliffs at Beachy Head. After his letter they had been convinced that they would find him dead. We all were. But his courage must have failed him, just as it had let him down on the night that Judy died. He was sitting in the driver's seat with a bottle of whisky in his hand. There were other empty bottles in the back. He was very cold, apparently, and not at all coherent.

The forensic evidence didn't contradict what he said happened that night eight years ago. It didn't confirm it either. The police were still considering whether they could justify an arrest.

Rosemary, the chairperson, had suggested that the funeral focus on Judy's life and comment on her death. She suggested that the eight years of uncertainty weren't really part of anything.

The police inspector, whose name turned out to be Robbins, gave a short talk about the importance of knowing about the end of Judy's short life. She had been the victim of a car accident, he said. Nothing more, nothing less. It was almost certain that she had been killed instantaneously. She hadn't known a thing, he said. She had given her family five delightful years and we must hold on to that. In many ways we were a lucky family.

It seemed a strange choice of word, and yet I had heard it used about my family before. This time it was meant in a different way. After years of horrible uncertainty, of not knowing whether Judy had been abducted, molested or murdered, we now knew the truth. We were never sure whether she had been alive for hours or days or even weeks after she disappeared, whether she had suffered anguish or pain, but now we knew. She had died immediately. This gave us immense comfort.

At the service some of the children from her class from all those years before were singing a song. I looked along the line at the faces. They were all thirteen, a little coy, possibly not really knowing why they were there, just responding to a call from a nice teacher from their old primary school. One of them was tall, almost my size I would say, while the others were all much shorter. A couple were plump and another downright thin. Most had modern hairstyles but one had hair right down her back with those wispy bits at the bottom so that it looked as though it had never been cut.

I wondered what my Judy would have been like. I put my hand up to my throat and felt her chain there. The letter "J" I held in my fingers. I thought then of the American girl and wondered where she was at that moment. I remembered Clare's advice: *Think of this American girl as a kind of symbol of your sister. A free spirit, travelling somewhere. Enjoying life.*

As the funeral moved on and the lady from the Humane Society asked us all to stand up and sing the last song, I pictured the American girl in an open-topped car speeding along a freeway in the USA. I had an image of wide open spaces, somewhere like the Grand Canyon. The land was a sort of mud colour and the sun sat like a giant orange in the sky. My American Judy was sitting in the passenger seat playing with the chain around her neck, the "J" slipping in and out of her mouth. Her mother, Margaret (an ex-FBI agent), was wearing dark glasses and driving with just one hand on the steering wheel, the other elbow leaning casually on the door.

I looked back to the tiny white coffin. Some velvet curtains were closing across the front of it and everyone was standing looking. I felt my dad's arm link with mine and I looked along the row to see my mum, Rosie, my dad and me all joined up.

As the coffin disappeared I closed my eyes, and I was back in America. Judy had her hands in the air, her hair flying out behind her, singing along to a song on the radio. In front of her was a long ribbon of road and on the horizon some big city full of possibilities.

That's how I wanted to remember her.